See You Soon

By M. Campos

See You Soon is a work of fiction. Names, characters, places, and incidents are the products of the author's imagination or are used fictitiously. Any resemblance to actual events, locales, or persons, living or dead, is entirely coincidental.

Copyright © 2025 by M. Campos
Illustration art by: Archaic Publications
Edited by: M.D.R

Printed in the United States of America

ARCHAIC
PUBLICATIONS

I SET SAIL INTO THE DARK, CAPSIZED UPSIDE DOWN
IN YOUR HEART.

See You Soon

CHAPTER ONE

Year: 2079 — Samuel

No matter what I do, I can't save her. No matter what I change, she dies again. It feels as though I've become a slave to time and death, yet the agony of reliving her demise—over and over—is worth *even* the slightest chance at a reality with Juliette in it. When I manage to alter the moment that leads to her death, within hours she slips from my grasp in some other tragic way.

The consequences ripple outward, touching people who never asked to be part of the design. Still, I don't care who else suffers for her sake. I would do anything for her. There is no depth I won't sink to for Juliette.

I'm not sure how I'm able to move through time—only that one variable in all this, or maybe several subtle ones working together, began with the storm's anomaly fusing with the circuitry of my phone and my IMC chip. Whatever the cause, I'm convinced that neither death nor life, neither angels nor demons, neither the past nor the future can separate me from her. I won't let it happen. As long as I can return to the past, I won't allow it.

This time I go back one day earlier. I pause, staring at the date glowing on my screen. It feels strangely formal, as if I'm agreeing to something without understanding the cost. My thumb hovers, then shifts the calendar back one square—a small, deliberate motion that somehow carries the weight of a much larger decision.

Light folds.

The world tilts the way it always does — not sharply, but with a soft, persistent pull, as if something patient has been waiting for me to follow. The air thins. Colors lose their edges. A faint stirring spreads from the IMC chip at the base of my skull — not painful, just unyielding, as if it's waking before I'm ready.

But it works. Once again, I'm reliving a day already lived. My life has become a throw of dice cast into an abyss of chance, with will and fate as my only gods.

I'm used to the uncertainty behind every change, yet the strain on my body grows heavier, the fatigue sharper. This chaos reminds me of an old, banned story I once found on the wire—a tale of a seventeenth-century sailor searching for his father who goes to war. The sailor drifts without

direction, lost both at sea and within himself, yet somehow
he always reaches where he needs to be. All the illegal
literature are the best reads.

"Last boarding call for terminal twelve-five-nine-one to
Kasper City, with permit routes to *Sokuke* and *Milwaukee City*."
The young woman's voice drifts over the telecom at the
metro station, clear and practiced.

As soon as I hear the announcement, a soft vibration pulses
through my IMC chip. A message. I pull out my phone, and
as before, Juliette's name lights the screen.

"Hey, Sam—are you on your way yet?" she asks, her voice
bright, almost electric.

"Yes, I'm about to board. It's good to hear from you. I miss
you." The words sound rehearsed even as I say them.

"Wow," she laughs. "I'd never expect that from you—not in
a million years, mister."

"You bring it out of me," I reply.

"I like that. Vibe me when you're near."

Her voice always does something to me. Each time I hear it,
it's like meeting her again for the first time. Every look, every
word, every small motion pulls me down to the bone of
what I am. She reminds me what it means to feel alive.

"Sir, please step this way if you're boarding," says the
attendant, gesturing me forward. I step onto the platform as
the full-body scan begins—efficient, soundless, precise. They

say there's no need to close your eyes anymore, but I still do. Maybe it's habit. Maybe it's the fear of what's new.

"Well done, sir. Now your ticket and New World Identification card."

"Here you go."

"Everything is up to date. Welcome aboard, Samuel Pine. Enjoy your trip."

I still hate the part where they hold your identification card until twenty minutes before arrival. Once, I didn't get mine back until the last minute. It's a helpless feeling, being nameless, even briefly.

After half an hour, one of the transport staff walks through the aisle with a scanner in hand.

"Samuel Pine?"

"That's me."

"Hello, I'm Delores. Tilt your head back, please."

As she lifts the device, I'm already moving. A hum passes through my eye, then my IMC chip. Not normal—but I say nothing. Probably another aftereffect from the electrical storm. The less attention I draw, the safer I stay.

Juliette plans an outing today—friends, the city, the same familiar walk. I know I should stop her. I remember what's coming. We survived it once, but I won't risk another mistake. *Kasper City* will be one of the first to fall when the meteorites hit tonight. That much I know.

The link slows to a halt. The same announcement plays again, just as it did before.

"You have arrived at *Kasper City*. Thank you for choosing Magnetic Transport."

"ALERT: MESSAGE: STAGE FIVE TORNADO WARNING. PLEASE AVOID MAJOR CITIES FOR YOUR SAFETY."

Even now, I can't make sense of that warning. How could they mistake meteor impacts for a tornado? It's absurd. But people believe what they need to. Some will understand when the ground shakes; but most won't care until the sky opens.

I call Juliette as I step off the link. Two rings this time, not four.

"Hey, just getting off?"

"Yeah. I'll see you soon."

"Okay, I'll be waiting outside. Ten minutes or so. Bye!"

I can't fail again. I just can't.

This time I rent a magnetic glide instead of walking. I ride straight to the jewelry shop—the old one, *The Eldest*. I don't even hesitate. If there's one thing I'm sure of, it's Juliette.

Inside, I find *the* ring. Eighteen-karat gold, ruby center, diamonds scattered like a constellation. I use every credit I have in savings—rent, bills, all that don't matter. No modern nanotech ring, this one is real. It gives me hope. Maybe this time, everything will be different.

"She's a lucky girl," says the automated service woman.

"No," I tell her. "I'm the lucky one."

"Have a nice day. Come back on *World United Week*—we'll have specials on everything."

I slip the ring into my jacket pocket. As I ride through the city toward Juliette, the air feels different. There's a static in it, faint but alive. People move slower, unaware of the stillness gathering around them. Unaware of what's coming.

I see her up ahead, combing her jet-black hair with her hands like she always does. I make it just in time.

"Hey rebel, can I get a lift?" she asks, smiling.

"Hold on, tiger."

She climbs on and wraps her arms around me, her head resting against my back. I almost tell her to cancel our plans, but when I feel her excitement — brighter than the last time — I change my mind. Let her have this day. Let me have it too.

We ride through the lower district, the hum of the glide soft beneath us. Juliette presses closer, her laughter scattering through the wind.

"Did you get that alert message from the national officials too?" she asks.

"I did. Just ignore it."

I'm already thinking about where I'll take her when the time comes to ask the question.

The Top of Nebula—safe ground and, in its way, romantic. Decent climb, gravitational stones, the ocean and the alpine stretching out beyond them. Few places like it remain since the comet of '52 twisted the world's magnetic poles. They say in twenty years the floating rocks will fall back to earth, and that will be the end of the wonder.

"Sam, turn left up here," Juliette whispers in my ear.

"Why?"

"It's a surprise. You'll like it," she says, pressing her body against me.

That's the thing about changing the past: it splits the paths ahead until they feel countless — some good, some terrible, most beyond anything I can predict.

"Okay," The word leaves me before I think too much about it.

She guides me into a narrow lane. "Close your eyes. No peeking."

"What's the surprise?"

"You'll see. Just trust me."

Her hand finds mine and tugs me forward. I let her lead. With anyone else I would resist, but not her.

"Open your eyes, Sam."

A tattoo parlor. Neon letters buzz above the door.

"I want matching tattoos," she says. "I already booked us and paid for the permits. Come on."

I can guess the chain of cause and effect that brings us here—the earlier call, the words that set her mind spinning.

"What are we getting?" I ask as we pass a wall of designs.

Juliette walks backward, smiling. "King and Queen of Hearts, Mr. Pine."

I've never thought about tattoos. I once considered laser graphics, the kind that change with a thought and erase with a touch. Permanent ink feels archaic, dangerous. But she's certain.

"I'll go first," I murmur.

"Don't be silly. I checked this place out. Just relax," she says, rising on her toes to kiss me.

Juliette sits first. The artist—Quail—is older, his neck inked with his own name.

"This'll sting a bit," he says. "Small piece, though. Won't be bad."

"Nice to meet you, Quail," Juliette tilts her head, amused. "I know your name; I did my research."

He laughs, adjusting his tools.

"Why your name?" I ask.

"Old habit," he says. "I'm old-fashioned."

"Quail's your last name?"

"No, first."

"I thought people used to ink their last names."

"That doesn't sound right," he says, laughing again. "All right, here we go."

The sound of the needle fills the room—a high, metallic whine like a dentist's drill from another era. Juliette squeezes my hand, wincing, then laughing through it. Ten minutes later it is done: a red heart beneath a crowned Q. Beautiful. Sharper than any laser mark I've ever seen.

"Thank you! It looks so gravity!" Juliette says, beaming.

"You're welcome," Quail grins. "Now you, with the K and the crown."

Before I can answer, the telecom blares:

"ALERT: MESSAGE: STAGE FIVE TORNADO WARNING. PLEASE AVOID MAJOR CITIES FOR YOUR SAFETY."

"Not this again," Juliette grumbles.

"Propaganda," Quail says. "Ignore it."

The reminder of what's coming lingers in the air. Still, when he finishes my tattoo, I slip a small tip, all I can manage. Seeing our marks side by side—her Q and my K—moves me more than I expect.

Outside, she looks up at me, eyes bright. I can't hold it back any longer.

"Hey," I say, taking her by the shoulders, my hands sliding down to hers.

"Hey back," she says with a shy smile.

"You're a beautiful person in every way," I say quietly. "Juliette Parker, I love you. I'm deeply in love with you."

She doesn't hesitate. "I love you too, Samuel Pine."

She kisses me. We break apart before the city drones fines us for the public display of affection.

"Thank you for the tattoo," I lift my arm a little. "One of many to come?"

"You're welcome," she laughs. "But no—too painful."

I wait to say the words, fearing they'll make losing her harder. Maybe the words themselves are what the universe needs to change its course. Maybe this time, that cliché is true.

We drift back into the main square to meet Juliette's friends. Two of them have just become a couple, proud and awkward in their new closeness. When Juliette mentions our matching tattoos, it sets something off between Allison and Russel; they slip away soon after, lost in their own orbit.

"I'm going to die utterly alone," Violet says. "Whoever I hang out with, I'm always the third or fifth wheel."

"Don't worry," Juliette says. "We'll find you someone tonight."

"I'm counting on it. Make sure he's rugged, with sharp features, dangerous eyes," Violet teases. "Sam, why don't you have any friends for me?"

"He doesn't need any," Juliette says, wrapping her arms around me. "He has me."

"You two are disgusting," Violet laughs. "All right, enough about you. Let's find me a man."

"ALERT: MESSAGE: STAGE FIVE TORNADO WARNING; PLEASE AVOID MAJOR CITIES FOR YOUR SAFETY."

"What nonsense," Violet says.

"Probably a bad joke," Juliette adds. "Are you getting these alerts too?"

"I am. It's constant. Makes me want to rip out my IMC."

They walk ahead, talking. Above Orion's belt, pale neon-gold sparks drift downward, unhurried, as if waiting for someone to look up. I watch them for a beat before we slip into the city lights. We spend the next hour drifting from bar to bar, the three of us playing at normalcy. Violet is the loudest, gathering eyes and laughter wherever she moves. She meets a man named Dave at the *Lit Bar*, and for a brief moment, her face softens as if something lifts from her.

When she ignores a direct call from her parents—one I remember clearly from before—I feel a chill. In the last loop, that call sends her home to safety. This time, she stays.

"Hey Juliette," I say softly. "There's a place I want to take you. Come on—let's go."

"After this mojito." She smiles. "Then I'm all yours. Oh — what about Violet?"

"She'll be fine," I reply.

"She can come with us."

"If she wants to."

Juliette turns. "Violet, we're taking off. You coming?"

"No, I'm staying here with Dave."

"We're going to *The Top of Nebula*," I tell her.

"Always wanted to go there," Juliette says, finishing her drink.

"Maybe later," Violet says. "We'll catch up."

I take Dave aside. "If you two don't go, take her across the street to the *Rocket Café*. It's safer there."

"Is she your family or something?" he asks, smirking. "Something like that." I step in closer, just enough to make him look away.

"Total gravity," he mutters, guiding her out.

"Everything good?" Juliette asks, resting her chin on my arm.

"I hope so. Let's go."

I've learned not to force outcomes. The more I push, the more the world seems to push back. In one loop they ship me off for cerebral therapy for months plus a fine. In another, they take my phone and leave me to navigate the day blind. I can't risk either again.

Outside, the sky is stirring—bands of emerald and sapphire threading through the dark like veins under skin. People stop where they are, lifted by the colors, murmuring to each other as if witnessing a blessing. But I know better. What they're admiring is the quiet warning, the soft prelude to the end as it begins to reach for us.

"Come on," I say quietly. "We should keep moving."

"What do you think it is?"

"Can't say. We'll see more from higher ground."

"It's beautiful."

"I'm carrying you." I lift her before she can protest. She laughs, unaware that I'm already moving faster than a walk. By the time we reach the mag-glide, I've shifted her in front of me, settling her against the handle wheel so she won't slip when we tear through the still streets.

"Something feels strange," she says. "Should we go back for Violet?"

"She'll be fine. Shoot her a vibe—tell her to get to Nebula. Same for Allison and Russel."

"I'll check if they're home first."

"Good," I reply.

She looks back at me. "Sam, what's going on?"

"I'll explain when we reach the top. I promise."

She doesn't press further. She never does when I say it like that.

By the time we reach the ridge, the air has thinned into a soft shimmer. Juliette walks ahead of me, turning back with that quiet expectancy, waiting for whatever truth I've been holding onto.

"There's something I need to ask you as well," I clear my throat, leading her past the floating gravity stones to a level patch of earth.

"I want the truth, Sam," she says, pulling her hand free.

Last time, she didn't believe me. She thinks I've broken under the pressure of life, and she has me committed in a psyche ward. Even then, she never leaves my side. I tell her about the meteorites, the river, her death—but it never matters.

I point upward. "Those lights aren't storms. They're celestial burns from the meteors that are going to hit. I don't know how long it will last—I've never lived past tomorrow. I go back every time you die, Juliette. Every time. It's been almost a month of looping the same days. That's why I know you so well. That's why I can say I love you without hesitation."

She stands silent, trembling, hands clasped together.

"I believe you," she says finally, and steps forward to hug me. "Of course I believe you. How are you doing it?"

"I'm not sure. When the meteors begin to fall, the air takes on a pulse of its own—something mechanical, something electrical—and it jolts my IMC awake. I trigger a reset through the chip to stabilize the system, but if I select a date before it locks, it pulls me through. The first time, it happened on its own."

She nods slowly. "That's a lot to take in, but I know you're telling the truth."

"It's starting soon," I sigh. "We'll feel quakes before we see the sky break."

"Is that why Violet should be here?"

"Or at the *Rocket Café*. That's where we survive before."

"She's there," Juliette whispers. "She sent me a vibe."

"I'm glad." I sit beside her, letting our shoulders be our reminder that we're not alone.

We watch the colors ripple above us, then fade into the darkness of falling stone. I tell her everything—from the first loop to yesterday, which is tomorrow for her.

The ground trembles beneath us.

She shivers. "You really do love me, don't you?"

"With everything I am," I take out the ring with steady hands. "Juliette Parker, will you marry me?"

"Yes."

The word hovers between us, weightless as a breath not yet released. I look into her coffee-colored eyes, her long jet-black hair drifting like ink, and for the first time since the storm, I feel fate loosen its grip on me.

Before I can guide the ring onto her finger, the air splits—sharp, metallic, certain of itself. Something small and merciless finds her chest, a fragment of meteorite cutting through before either of us can understand what's happened.

Juliette's breath catches. She leans into me a little more, the way someone does when they're listening closely or steadying their balance. For a heartbeat she is right there, warm against my side. I only hold her, feeling the warmth leave her body as fire swallows the city below.

The screams rise to the mountaintop and then thin out, carried off by the wind until only the crash of waves against stone remains.

Of all the realities I've crossed, this pain is the one that settles deepest. Something in me goes quiet, and I know it won't return.

When dawn comes, I bury Juliette on that mountain—my heart beside hers. After that, I stop believing in salvation.

CHAPTER TWO

Year: 1999 — Markus

T he sound of my alarm clock arrives the way morning light does—whispering through the blinds, brushing across my face, gentle and patient but insistent. I know what it means and still, I ignore it. The last month of the fall semester has drained me. Not from the schoolwork—I'm ahead in every class—but from working nights at the galvanizing plant. I'll be full-time soon. The thought doesn't comfort me.

It's not that my life is terrible. It's that it feels decided — like someone else wrote it before I was born.

"Markus, wake up!" my aunt shouts from the doorway. "You're going to be late *again*!"

"I'm up," I mutter, rolling out of bed into my morning pushups.

I have plans, or at least ideas. College can wait. Aunt Carol and I need stability first—a year at most, I tell myself. We've been bouncing between relatives for too long, each place warm at first, cold by the third month. You can always tell when a home stops wanting you.

The last place wasn't terrible—cramped, sure, and the meals thin—but it was the first time in a while I could breathe. I found my job there and saved what I could. Carol didn't like the idea of me postponing college, but she didn't stop me either. Maybe she understood. Maybe she wanted her own corner of peace too—like the one we lost after the accident took my parents and everything that belonged to us.

"I'll see you this evening," she turns to me, her keys jingling. "They're delivering furniture today — a dresser for you too."

"I'll be here."

"Maybe you can ask some friends to help."

"I don't have any friends," I say flatly. "Not anymore."

Sometimes people just fade apart. Other times, it's one mistake that changes everything. Mine was that party. The night my parents died. Carol says I shouldn't feel guilty — that it's what saved me — but I don't believe that. I could've done something. I should've.

Since then, the world has quieted around me. I see people differently now — not as friends or strangers, but as risks. Mistakes waiting to happen.

"Markus!" Carol calls again.

"What?"

"I'll pick up food after work — just make sure you get more water!"

"I'm on foot, Carol."

She laughs as the door shuts behind her.

Everyone's been on edge lately — *Y2K* panic spreading through the neighborhood like static. Carol and I have been stocking up on canned goods, bottled water, even medicine. I don't believe in all that, but if it keeps her calm, I'll stack cans until the shelves give out.

When I step outside, the morning looks off. There's a strange tint in the sky — cedar green in patches, like bruised glass.

"Markus, where's your aunt going?" Mrs. Paige, my next-door neighbor, asks from her porch.

"She's at work."

"You two should stay inside," she says nervously. "Look at the sky, child — it's that *Y2K*! I'm going back in."

"Lock your door, Mrs. Paige."

The street hums with quiet hysteria. Some people stand frozen, staring up; others rush through the day pretending nothing's wrong. The green fades to a lilac haze, then a bruised red. I stop without meaning to, caught in it, until movement around me pulls me back to earth.

At the corner of Bishop Avenue, it hits me — a sudden separation, like my body and mind no longer belong to each other. Elastic. Empty. Then it passes, leaving me weak and dizzy.

Probably low blood sugar, I tell myself. Nothing cosmic. Nothing strange.

But when I reach the warehouse, I stop cold.

The entire assembly line — all of it — is on the opposite side of the building.

"Markus, I need you to take the new hire and show her around. Train her too," Mike, the warehouse manager, says, flipping through his clipboard. "Also, you're late — but there's a first time for everything. I'll let it slide, champ."

"What?"

"What do you mean, what?" He gives me that look — half grin, half disbelief. "You asked for a supervisory role yesterday, remember? Here's your shot. Prove yourself." Then he calmly walks into his office before I can respond.

A girl stands up and approaches, her hair a cool blonde, pulled tight reaching her hips, eyes sharp gray and curious. "Hi, I'm Lindsay. Nice to meet you."

"Hi," I say, shaking her hand automatically. "I'm Markus. This is… strange."

"What's *strange*?"

"This place. It's all different."

She glances around. "Now that you mention it, yeah — it does look different since last time I was here."

"When was that?"

"A few days ago. Thursday. Orientation."

"I need to look around," I mutter. "Something's off."

"Okay," she says carefully. "I'll follow you; I guess."

Everything has changed. The machines are rearranged, bolted in new positions — only there are no bolts, no marks, no sign they were ever anywhere else. I ask a few coworkers, but they just laugh, thinking I'm trying to impress the new girl.

It makes no sense. You can't move a whole assembly overnight — not without leaving a trace.

"Is this a prank?" I ask under my breath.

"I don't know what you're talking about," Lindsay says, though her brow furrows.

"I've been late every day since I got hired," I mutter. "There's no way Mike would trust me to train anyone."

Just then, Derek from HR strolls over — except Derek isn't our HR guy. "Morning, Markus. Morning, Lindsay. Here's your ID badge," he says, handing it over. "Oh, and your direct deposit is set up. You're good to go."

"Thanks," Lindsay says.

"And congrats on the trainer promotion, Markus. You'll do great."

"Uh—thank you, sir."

When he walks off, I whisper, "This is odd. Very odd."

"What happened to Jake?" Lindsay asks suddenly.

"Who's Jake?"

"The HR who hired me."

I stare at her. "Derek's the only HR we've got."

For a moment, doubt gnaws at me. Maybe I'm losing it. But then I see it in Lindsay's face — confusion giving way to fear.

"Okay, this is getting strange—" she starts, but the sentence breaks in half as the ground begins to shake.

The quake hits hard.

Rolling through the floor like a living thing.

We dive under the restroom doorway, metal groaning overhead. Cages burst open. Bolts rain down. For almost a minute, the whole building convulses. Then, silence.

No one moves for a long time. When the foreman finally shouts roll call, we file out into the parking lot.

Outside, the sky is calm. Blue. Ordinary.

"I wonder what happened to all the colors," Lindsay murmurs, scanning the clouds.

"I don't know."

I turn to a few coworkers. "Hey Fred, Tim—what do you make of the weird colors this morning?"

They stare at me blankly.

"What colors?" Fred asks.

"Nothing," I say quickly, forcing a laugh. "Just messing around."

I turn back to Lindsay. "We need to leave."

"Why?"

"I don't know," I admit. "Something's wrong. Some people notice it, others don't. That's the part that scares me."

We walk past the loading dock — and that's when I notice the light. The shadows are wrong. They're bending slightly *toward* the sun, like reflections that forgot which direction to obey. The pavement ripples faintly underfoot, but no one else seems to feel it.

The silence that follows is deep, like the world's breath caught in its throat.

A soundless pulse rolls through the air — not an aftershock, something else — and I swear the sky flickers for half a heartbeat, a mirror catching light from nowhere.

"Markus?" Lindsay's voice is faint. "Are we okay?"

I open my mouth to answer, but the air thickens, like invisible static pressing on my eardrums.

Then everything snaps back to normal.

I tell Mike we're heading out. He barely objects, says we can all clock out early while they check for damage. "Safer that way," he says. He's calmer than I've ever seen him — another detail that doesn't fit.

"I'll drive," Lindsay offers. "I saw you walking earlier. But I need to stop at my grandparents' first."

"That's fine."

On the way, I keep glancing at the sky — waiting for the strange glow to return — but everything looks deceptively normal.

Except it isn't. Traffic lights pulse slightly out of rhythm. A billboard resets every few seconds like a broken signal loop. The air smells faintly metallic — like burnt copper.

"So, you live with your grandparents?" I ask.

"Yeah. My real parents are gone."

"I'm sorry."

She shrugs. "How would you know? It was a long time ago — I was nine."

"My parents are gone too," I say quietly. "Last year."

Her tone softens. "How?"

"There was an accident. Power lines malfunctioned — took out half the block."

"I remember that. The news said a dozen homes were lost."

"More than that," I say. "They offered us settlement money. We didn't take it."

"I wouldn't have either."

"What about your parents?" I ask, steering the conversation away.

"They just left," she says, almost laughing. "Dropped me off one summer and never came back. I guess they're dead. Or maybe they just stopped existing in the part of the world that includes me."

"Well," I say, "good riddance."

"Good riddance indeed."

She smiles — that strong, matter-of-fact kind of smile that hides years of adaptation. She has presence — firm handshake, steady voice, unflinching eyes. The kind of person who doesn't crumble easily.

When we reach her house, she tells me to wait in the car so her grandparents won't get the wrong idea. I recline the seat and watch her walk up the porch steps. Then she freezes.

"Lindsay?" I call, as I approach her.

"The door." Lindsay states. "It isn't the same door. The old red one is gone — replaced by some beige frame and the floral mat."

 The current mat reading *Sweet Home.*

She fumbles with her keys, the wrong metal scratching at the wrong lock.

Then we both hear it — the click of the door unlocking from the inside.

And the face that appears isn't her grandparents.

"Lindsay, are you trying to break the door?"

"Mom?" Lindsay stares, then lunges forward and hugs her, sobbing into her shoulder.

"Are you okay, sweetie? And who's this handsome young man?"

"Hello. I'm Markus Brentfern," I answer, hovering in the doorway, unsure whether to offer my hand.

"Ruth Thomas," she says warmly. "Lindsay's mother. Nice to meet you."

"When did you get back? Is Dad here too?" Lindsay wipes her eyes.

"He should be home soon. He had to run an errand." Ruth studies her. "What's going on with you?"

"I haven't seen you in almost a decade. That's what's wrong."

"Haven't seen me…? We had breakfast together this morning. Are you on drugs? Did this boy give you drugs?" Her eyes snap to me. "You stay away from my daughter, you hear!"

"Are you insane?!" Lindsay shouts.

"We're just kidding, Mrs. Thomas. A prank," I say quickly, palms up. "We saw something like it on TV—thought we'd try it. Right, Lindsay?" I give her a small, desperate wink.

"That's right. A joke. Sorry, Mom." Lindsay forces a smile.

"Well, good job, both of you. I was about to call the cops," Ruth says, stepping back inside. "Come to the kitchen. I made cookies."

I lean toward Lindsay. "I know this is crazy, but if we play along, we can ask questions."

"Screw this. I want to leave." She turns for the car. I follow.

"What about your grandparents? You wanted to check on them." I hold out my hand. "We ask what we need, then we go—forever, if that's what you want. We're in this together."

She looks at my hand, then takes it. "Okay." As our fingers lock, I let myself imagine—for one breath—that my parents might be alive somewhere too.

Inside, everything is different. Even her bedroom. Different paint, different furniture, different life. When Lindsay realizes none of her grandparents' things are in the house, panic breaks over her.

"Their stuff isn't here, Markus. Their bedroom is somebody's office." Her voice shakes.

"Stay calm. I'll ask your mom about them so it sounds natural."

"She's not my mother. And this isn't my room!" Lindsay grabs a trophy from the shelf. "Look at this. Tennis. I don't play tennis." Her certainty is absolute.

"This isn't your home," I say softly. "I get it. Something's wrong—like the warehouse."

"This is bizarro world. I need to find my grandparents now." She moves for the door. I catch her arm.

"Think for a second. Either they don't belong here, or we don't. If we're the ones out of place, we shouldn't provoke the people who think nothing's wrong." I soften my voice.

"She may not be the mother who left you. She's probably not your mother at all. But to *her*, you're a daughter she cares about."

"Ask about my grandparents so we can leave," she says, yanking free. The old wound is wide open; abandonment does that. You can stitch it closed with forgetting, but the first memory that returns tears it all again.

"Remember—we're in this together," I add, and pull her into a hug. She doesn't resist. Her jaw trembles against my chest, and I hold her until it stops.

We sit at the kitchen table while Ruth works a new batch of dough.

"There you two are. Have some of my famous butterscotch cookies." Lindsay flicks her eyes at me: *ask*.

"Lindsay invited me to visit her grandparents later," I say when Ruth sets the plate down. "Is that all right?"

"Of course," Ruth says, then her smile falters and resets. "And please—call me Ruth."

"Could you tell me a bit about them?"

"They were very loving," Ruth says, returning to the counter. "I miss them so—"

As she speaks, tears begin slipping down Lindsay's face. She stands and walks out without a word.

"Thanks for the cookies, Ruth! Mind if we take them to go?" I wrap most of the batch in a paper towel, more for courtesy than appetite. "It was nice meeting you!"

"It was nice meeting you too, Markus," Ruth calls. "Make sure she watches the road!"

By the time I reach the driveway, a car is pulling in. A man steps out — her father. Lindsay sits rigid behind the wheel, terrified and hollow. I slide into the passenger seat, waving hello as he approaches—too late to avoid him.

"Hey! Where are you going?" he asks, crouching to see me.

"To visit her grandparents," I reply, looking down.

"Oh." He looks down too. "Drive safe, Lindsay."

"Dad?"

"Yeah, sweetie?"

"I love you," she says.

"I love you too." He taps the roof twice and turns away.

I don't speak for most of the drive. I remember what I wanted when I heard about my parents: silence. Even so, I hold her hand. Sometimes you need proof that you are not entirely alone, even when you think you want to be.

"Markus?" she says at last, tears streaking.

"Yeah?"

"What the hell is going on?"

"I don't know. But we'll find out. I promise."

"How?"

"We can't be the only ones. We'll find others like us." I squeeze her hand. "I just hope my aunt is still *my* aunt."

"If my grandparents are dead in this place, that means we're the ones who don't belong here, right?"

"I'd assume so. Once we reach my aunt, we plan the next step."

We check my apartment first; she isn't there. Lindsay comes upstairs with me—neither of us wants to split. With no sign of Carol, we head for her workplace. I've only been there once; she hated it. "Training," she said. "No visitors." Today I have a reason she can't ignore.

As we slide back into the car, a sharp electrical sting jumps through us both — like a static shock, but larger, deeper. It vanishes as fast as it hits. Then the sky changes.

The morning's strange colors return, brighter, and above them hangs a *translucent, upside-down city*. We step out of the car, staring. A soldier — borderline transparent, in full military kit — sprints straight toward us.

I throw myself in front of Lindsay, but before he reaches us, he blinks out — still in motion — and is gone. No trace except the static that lifts every hair on our arms. Lindsay's hair stands wild, as if charged from within.

"I need to get to my aunt," I press. She is frozen, so I guide her back into the car, buckle her in, and take the wheel. The sky is unrecognizable now. Everyone sees it — heads up, mouths open, traffic stalled as people flood the streets to watch the floating city and the slow rivers of color above.

When the roads lock, we are half a block from Carol's workplace. We run.

"Keep up, please!" I shout, weaving through bodies.

"I'm trying!" she pants.

At Decanter and Morris Lane, I see my aunt outside looking up with everyone else. Relief hits me — then vanishes. Heat rolls across the intersection, joined by the same electrical pressure — and then the buildings ahead erupt. A shockwave takes our legs. More explosions follow. Through smoke and grit, I understand; meteorites are slamming into the city, one after another.

I run toward where my aunt had been; Lindsay clings to my shirt as I stumble through bodies. I find Carol. I know it's her even before I can fully see her.

I sit beside her and stare at the torn bodies all around us. Lindsay tugs and calls my name but I can't hear. Above us, stones scream through the air. The sky is color and fire and the ghost of the upside-down city.

"Markus! We have to move!" Lindsay slaps me hard enough to crack the trance. We run — no plan, only away — until the fires thin. Then more strikes fall ahead and I drag her into the alleys, keeping to narrow ways where fewer people clog our path. Half a mile on, the impacts fade. Our legs fail. We walk.

"Do you think it's the end of the world?" she asks.

"It could be," I say honestly.

"What do we do now?"

"We go somewhere familiar and safe, my place — until we figure something out." I answer.

"We should go to the cops. Tell them everything."

"Tell them what? That the world is out of joint? That people we love are alive and dead depending on which way you turn? They'll lock us up for being crazy."

"Everything that's happening *is* crazy. What does it matter?"

"Let's go back to my place. Then we decide," I say, soft but firm.

"Fine. Whatever you say." She exhales, then glances at me. "I'm sorry about your aunt."

"She's still alive," I counter. "And so are your grandparents — just not here."

We fall quiet, walking under the wounded sky. She whispers — prayer or instinct, I can't tell. Near my building where we saw the military man, the static returns — violent this time, a halo of crackling air around us. We can't move. A low hum rises and keeps rising until it is almost a blade.

Light. A flash like the sun opening its eye.

Then we are somewhere else. A facility — white, metallic, humming — and before I can understand what I am seeing, hands slam me against a wall.

Chapter Three

Year: 2079 — Samuel

I feel like talking to my parents. They are not around anymore, but I decide to visit them anyway. As much as I want to try to save Juliette again, I feel obligated to speak to my mother and father. Coincidentally, I can only travel back to January 1, 2079—the day they are buried. That is as far as I can go.

Unfortunately, no one in my time has full access to a calendar anymore. Every phone's calendar is limited. I can only travel as far back as the calendar system allows me, restricted by what I manage to acquire.

Almost everything is regulated now—even history. The few history books still in circulation are scrubbed clean, and anything older requires a permit to read. Reruns of factual programs, old vlogs, commercials, and news archives beyond a few years are hidden away. It is not illegal to know the past, just inconvenient. To access recorded history, you need a hall permit, a screen monitor pass, and another permit to check out any physical copies. Even then, the material is monitored, and visual requests only yield transcripts. And no matter what permits I get, I cannot upload older calendars into my IMC chip.

Time travel starts simple enough: select a date, initiate a reset, brace for the surge. A flash floods through the brain—an electrical storm from the Internal Magnetic Circuit chip—and then the vertigo hits. It is like waking mid-paralysis, trapped between breath and dream, until the light returns and the body catches up. My limbs always feel weak afterward, as though sleep and gravity are fighting inside me.

As the world blurs, I catch one last glimpse of Juliette's grave. The ground ripples and folds in on itself, the flames vanish, and fog rolls across the sky like a curtain falling on the past. When the haze clears, I stand near home again, numb to everything. I take a rented magnetic glide and head for my parents' cemetery, walking the last miles out of respect. They hated machines; walking feels right.

When I step onto the graveyard path, the tears come without warning. I kneel between their stones and cry until my throat burns and my body trembles. All the pressure I have been carrying cracks open there. When it passes, I feel light—

empty but balanced. I lie between them and watch the sunset bleed out across the clouds. For the first time in weeks, I feel peace.

I tell them about Juliette. About how she stayed home when I was sick, how she made tea and cleaned my fridge, how she laughed at my expired food. We talked all night back then. That is when I fell for her, though I did not know it. I tell my parents about everything since she died, every broken moment since. I do not expect an answer. I just need them to listen. Wherever they might be.

The sky dims, almost without notice, as though the light has decided to withdraw. The cemetery is closing; after dark, entry comes with a price and the quiet presence of watchful eyes. I rise, slightly unsteady, but calmer than I expect, the feeling settling in my chest like cooled embers.

Near the exit, a young man leans against a stone pillar beside a grave marked by a small fountain. The water moves faintly, steady and indifferent. He studies me for a moment and then smiles. There is nothing hurried in it. Nothing kind. Only a sense that he knows something I do not.

"Beautiful, isn't it?" he says. "The setting sun. Such poetry can only be appreciated at a distance."

I have not heard him approach.

"Yeah, I suppose," I say, and make my way to sit on the commune bench.

"Waiting for the magnetic bus?"

"No. Just collecting my thoughts."

He nods, watching the approaching bus.

"Fascinating, isn't it," he says. "How technology has evolved since '52. The birth of magnetic pulse travel. It's all quite gravitational."

He smiles, boards, and is gone. For a moment I wonder if he has ever been there at all. He looks frail, yet something about him makes the air tighten—the kind of quiet power that makes you forget your own size.

I walk home through the city, slow and deliberate, letting the night close around me. The streets murmur with distant traffic and dim windows, but I keep my eyes forward, my thoughts pared down to the simple act of moving. By the time I reach our place, the calm has thinned into something tired and brittle.

Inside, my roommate sits on the couch with a drink in his hand, the soft glow of the television washing his face in dull light. He barely looks up. The air smells faintly of alcohol and old fabric, familiar and unchanged.

"Yo," Jex says, tossing me a beer. "Thought you were going to your aunt and uncle's."

"I decided to visit my parents instead."

"But we were just there this morning."

"I know. I had more to say."

"Sorry, man. Didn't mean to sound insensitive. You doing okay?"

"I'm better now," I say, sitting beside him. "So, no work?"

"Got fired," he says without remorse. "They didn't like that I missed yesterday. Doesn't matter. Got interviews lined up already."

"Don't sweat it. You can do better anyway."

"Of course," he says, with a small smirk. "But maintenance work's dead-end stuff."

"You worked maintenance for multiple companies, didn't you?"

"Yeah. One of them was the Transmission of Internal Magnetic Circuit," he says, a little proud. "Expanded my memory storage there. Recovered old games, lost prints. Even old impulse designs."

On the screen, a documentary plays: *The Beginning of Magnetism in America.* I think of the stranger at the cemetery.

"Yo, I heard a theory," Jex says, sinking deeper into the couch. "Ever since that comet in '52, we've been drifting out of orbit. That's why lunar data's unstable. The scientists can't predict full moons anymore."

"Where'd you hear that?"

"The science channel. Same one we're watching. And the unknown statics. People panicked when the comet was coming in. Some offed themselves. Governments argued about what to do. You can lose days on conspiracy threads about it."

"What else do you know about the orbit shift?" I ask.

"Not much to it other than that," he says. "Space rock knocked us off our orbit, like a magnet pushing another magnet." He studies my face. "Sam, are you feeling okay?"

"I am. I'm just going through some things right now," I say. A small, sharp hope flickers in me. "But I need to ask you about your clearance at your old job."

"What about it?"

"Would it be possible to get us in so we can adjust my IMC chip's calendar? Make some modifications?"

"Not anymore. I was fired."

"Jex, I need to reach the year 2052."

He frowns, as if testing the words in his head. "Sorry, I thought you said you need to get to the year 2052."

"Forget what I said. Just tell me how to expand my calendar," I counter, my hand tightening on his arm.

He stares at me. "Everything is tied to your IMC number. A few voice commands, that's it. It's all done in the Transmission Seventy-Five room. Seriously, what's going on with you?"

"If I went in as you, would I have trouble with anyone?"

"I don't understand, Sam. Why would—"

"Just answer the question."

"Yeah, I'm sure," Jex says, getting to his feet. "Tell me what this is about."

"I have to make the impossible possible," I laugh. Explaining any more is pointless. To him it is theory. To me it is the shape of the day.

"Are you time traveling?" he asks. "How?"

"Mechanically speaking," I answer, "it's a high electrical surge from my IMC chip. From an anomaly in a storm."

"An anomaly," he repeats, with that crooked tone of his.

"Yes. An anomaly."

"You should apply at the *Gravity Tunes,*" I add, the certainty sudden and strange. "I have a strong feeling you'll like working there."

I pull out my phone and select.

"What are you trying to accomplish exactly, mate?"

"Forget what I said. I'm not even sure you'll remember this once I travel out," I counter, as the phone screen drops into black and the surge begins. My IMC buzzes.

Light fractures the room and time folds it.

As soon as the travel completes, I am back in my bed the way I was that morning. The same ceiling. The same dull light. The same weight in my chest. I decide to sleep a few hours before I go through with my plan.

About three hours before Jex wakes for his nine-a.m. shift, I walk into his room and take his work uniform from the chair. I head out to his job site on his magnetic glide, guided by the navigation tracker. I registered my fingerprint on his glide the day I rushed him to the hospital during what looked like a seizure. It turned out to be nothing, but the machine still remembers me.

Jex has the new generation of glides—the fastest on the market. They can autopilot at top speed. I still prefer manual steering. Machines drive without fear.

As I near the facility, I see how well manned it is. Patrols everywhere. Every entrance and exit guarded by at least four armed servicemen. They wave me through without question. Jex's glide must be familiar to them.

Inside the lobby, I move with a cluster of workers, slipping past the first line of checks without even lifting the keycard. For a moment I think that might be enough. Then I see the new full-body scanners looming ahead. My pulse jumps. I keep walking with everyone else, the line shuffling toward the humming gates. Sweat gathers at the back of my neck.

Some servicemen and even a few civilians bypass the main scanners, veering through side doors. I feel eyes settle on me. When I glance around, one guard is staring straight in my direction. I force my gaze back to the person stepping into the scan.

I pull out my phone and open the calendar. My thumb hovers just in case I need to disappear. That is when I notice a pair of maintenance workers slipping through a bronze door along the west wall.

With the phone still in my hand, I step out of the line and angle toward that door, falling in a few paces behind them, trying to match their pace.

I am halfway there when an administrator and an armed guard move in front of me like they have been waiting.

"Excuse me, sir," the administrator says. "Show me your physical identification bio."

I select the day prior on my calendar and initiate the reset. Or I believe I do. My thumb moves on reflex, too quick to correct, and I glance down just in time to see the error forming. January third instead of the first.

"Give me a few seconds," I say, forcing the smile to hold.

"Show me your identification," the administrator replies, voice flat, procedural. "Or we'll be forced to intervene." The guard beside him shifts, already prepared for the moment to break.

The hum begins behind my eyes, low and invasive. It spreads through my skull like pressure under deep water.

Then the light comes — not gentle, not kind — folding over the world as if reality itself is being pressed flat.

I rise from my bed as I do on January 3, 2079. This time there is no pause. No second-guessing. I take Jex's uniform and his glide and tear back toward the facility.

In the lobby, I move straight for the steel door I saw before. I do not make it halfway. Guards surge in from every direction, boots striking tile, voices sharp and closing.

I pull out my phone, deliberate now, and select January 1, 2079. As I run, the steel door waits ahead, the keycard reader gleaming beside it. I have nothing to offer it. An advanced building with an old lock. The irony lands even as I move. Almost funny.

I swing at the nearest guard as the reset takes hold and feel bone beneath my knuckles. Solid. Certain. It is a small comfort.

Once again, I am back on January 1, 2079, riding the rental glide toward my aunt and uncle's house.

I turn the glide around hard and head for home instead.

I take Jex's uniform and his keycard this time.

I take his glide again to avoid suspicion.

I walk down the west corridor of the facility, not hurrying, not lagging, toward the steel door I know is there.

I swipe the card. The light flickers green. The steel door opens.

I am *in*.

The hallways inside are a small labyrinth. I move through them quickly, searching for Transmission Seventy-Five. I expect the room numbers to follow some sequence. They do not. Some doors have no numbers at all. After enough blind lefts and rights, I find it: T75 stamped cold on the metal.

I swipe Jex's keycard again and slip inside.

The room is filled with monitors and coils and the quiet breath of machines. I climb onto the platform, connect the tubes and bands, and feel the buzz as my IMC chip links via wave pulse.

"INSERT YOUR AUTHORIZED KEYCARD," the operating system says.

I slide the card into the slot, hoping the system does not bother with identity analysis.

"WELCOME BACK, JEX TITOR."

"Transmission Seventy-Five, expansion required," I say. "Upload complete calendar into IMC chip number SP874211-667."

"REQUEST GRANTED. ALL OUTDATED CALENDARS UPLOADED."

"Thank you, Transmission Seventy-Five."

"YOU ARE WELCOME, SIR."

I disconnect from the system and pull out my phone. The calendar has changed. The dates stretch back and back, further than I need, further than anyone should touch. For a moment I just stare at it, feeling something like joy and dread tangled together.

Then the entrance door opens behind me with a hiss.

"What are you doing here?" a patroller says. His hand hovers near his weapon. "There is no scheduled run for this transmission at this hour." He steps closer. Using Jex's keycard has thrown some quiet flag.

"I am covering an emergency analysis of the operating system," I say. My voice stays steady. "I can show you my keycard and my bio information for clearance."

Out of the corner of my eye I glance at my phone. No pulse signal. Either it is an ugly coincidence, or someone has locked down transmissions in and out.

"Please do, sir," the patroller says. His shoulders ease just a little.

I walk toward him with the keycard in my hand, arm extended. When I am about two feet away, I let the card fall. He bends to pick it up.

I seize his shoulders and drive my knee into his face. His head whips back. He goes down hard.

I take his sidearm and his rifle from his vest.

I try the phone again. The signal is still dead.

In the corridor, more patrollers are already moving toward the door. I cannot say how many. Enough.

I have never fired a weapon with the intention to kill. That ends here.

I open fire. Two patrollers drop before they can react. The others fire back from both sides of the hall, bullets striking metal and wall. I duck behind the frame of the door and shoot blind around the corner, counting bursts and screams instead of faces. They go down in pieces, one after another.

"Sir, he's shooting back!" someone cries over a comm channel. Then only the ring of spent metal.

When the silence holds, I move. I sprint down the main corridor, heart pounding against my ribs. One last patroller steps into view and I shoot him without thinking. The rifle clicks empty. I toss it. The hallway stretches ahead like a throat.

If I can get to the roof, I might catch a clean signal. Either I disappear or I face more patrollers and, beyond them, the servicemen outside. I decide not to test that balance.

I run until I find a stairwell and take it two, three steps at a time.

At the top, I ease the door open and step into another corridor instead of open air. I start running again, phone in my hand.

That is when the air changes.

An electrical ray flickers across the corridor, and then another, and another, until the whole length of hall is a storm of color and distortion.

I keep running. About twenty feet ahead I see two silhouettes caught in the shimmer, like people on the far side of water. I pull the sidearm and fire a few rounds. As I get closer, my certainty falls away. They are not what I thought. I fire again anyway. The colors peel back and human shapes form under the light.

I squeeze the trigger once more. The gun clicks empty. I drop it and slam into the larger figure, pinning him against the wall beside a fire extinguisher.

"Who are you!?"

"What?" he manages.

"Leave him alone!" the other voice says. A woman. They both look terrified. They do not look like patrollers. They look like people who were walking somewhere else a minute ago.

I push the man down and run north along the corridor. No pulse signal yet. Panic scratches at the edge of my thoughts.

There is no roof access, no door that says EXIT, only more walls and more corners. I kick open a random office and grab a chair, hurling it at the window. The glass absorbs it and throws the chair back. Reinforced.

I hit it again. Nothing. There is nothing heavy enough in the room to matter.

I run back into the hall. The two strangers are still there, watching me, as if trying to decide which of us is real. I take the fire extinguisher from the wall and carry it back into the office. They follow.

I throw the extinguisher with everything I have. The glass cracks in a spiderweb. I throw it again and the window bursts outward, the shards falling into the dark.

A faint pulse signal flickers on my phone.

I lean out, holding the device toward the open sky, and initiate the travel sequence without allowing myself to consider where I am going. The air feels thinner here, as if the world has already begun to loosen around the edges.

"What is this place?" the man asks, stepping up behind me.

I do not turn at first. "Don't you work here?" I say, my voice calm, almost idle, as though the answer should already belong to him.

"We don't," the woman says. "We don't know what's going on. We were walking down Roscommon Street and then there was this electrical wave and now we're here."

I do not know if I believe them yet. Before I can answer, the calendar opens fully. I stab at a date in haste: January thirty-first, 2079, ten-thirty in the morning. I do not remember where I am at that time in this timeline. Wherever it is, it is not this corridor.

Light rises. The office dissolves.

When the world returns, I am in my bedroom.

I am on the floor. The two strangers are on their knees beside me, breathing like they have been drowning and just now broke the surface. It took me dozens of time-folds to stop collapsing that way.

"Markus," the girl says, clutching the man's arm.

"How are you two following me?" I ask. My voice sounds flat even to me. "Answer me or I'll kill you."

"I don't know!" the one called Markus replies. "We were looking for a safe place during the meteor chaos and we ended up here."

"We don't know what's going on," the girl says. "To what's happening. To why my parents seem to know who I am."

"Look, man," Markus says. "Lindsay and I don't want any trouble. We can leave right now."

"What year do you think it is?" I ask.

"It's 1999," Lindsay quickly answers. "December twenty-first, 1999."

I let out a slow breath. "I'm going to check on my roommate. If you need water, help yourselves in the kitchen. You're feeling like this because you time traveled to the year 2079. You'll feel like yourselves soon."

I am still sorting their words in my head as I walk down the hall. As much as I want to press them, I need to know where I stand in this altered line of days.

Jex is asleep on his bed, breathing deep. He has grown a beard. Small change. Proof that time has not left him untouched.

"Jex, wake up," I say, shaking his shoulder. "I need you to wake up."

He bolts upright when he sees me. "You have to get out of here," he says. "They're looking for you."

"I'm not surprised," I remark. "What I need to know is if you're okay." I need to see what my choices have done to everything that comes after.

"Yeah, I'm good," he says, swinging his legs off the bed. "They interrogated me for two weeks, but they let me go. How are you time traveling?"

"Mechanically speaking," I say, "it's a high electrical discharge from my IMC chip. From that storm anomaly."

"An anomaly," he says again, with the same small edge.

"Yes. An anomaly. I came to check on you and to know what my situation is. Now I'm leaving."

"Hold on, mate," Jex says as I move toward the door — with caution.

The two new arrivals are in the kitchen, on their feet, hunting for water they do not know how to find.

"I suppose in the year 1999 the water dispenser is not behind the marble square," I state. I press the stone, and the hidden fountain lowers. I fill two cups and hand them over. They drink like their throats are lined with dust.

"Who are these two?" Jex asks, stepping into the kitchen.

"This is Markus, and this is Lindsay," I respond. "From the year 1999."

Jex's eyebrows climb but he does not back away. "You two, sit down," he says, pulling chairs from the table. "You look worn out."

He starts asking them questions—where they were walking, what they saw in the sky, what the colors looked like. It gives me room to pull up every article and fragment I can find about the comet of 2052. I need to know all of it. Every theory. Every lie. Every gap.

I am glad Jex is a better host than I am. In moments that require manners, I tend to come up empty. His presence eases the room while Markus and Lindsay slowly come back to themselves. He seems more excited than afraid, which makes it easier for me to stay here and think instead of running straight back into the storm.

The questions move back and forth—Jex to Markus, Markus to Lindsay, Lindsay back to Jex. He has had nearly a month to live with the possibility of time travel; the idea has already chewed its way into his worldview.

"Sam," Jex says at last, stepping away from the table. "I don't think the safety tracker in your IMC chip is active. I'm almost certain the authorities would have been here by now if it were."

"Either way, my phone calendar is ready," I reply, leaning against the counter. "Just in case."
He studies me for a moment, the look saying everything — *so that's how you're doing it* — and nothing more.

"I'm trying to save Juliette," I say quietly. "All of this is for her."

"Standing columnar wave," Jex murmurs, half to himself, already drifting into theory. "It must be. Who's Juliette?"

"The girl I'm going to meet soon." I offer no further explanation. The silence does its work. He accepts it.

"Then just save her," he says, patting my shoulder in that awkward, almost brotherly way of his.

"That's the plan."
I glance down at my phone, then back at him. "That's why I'm going to destroy *The Great Comet of '52*."

Chapter Four

Year: 2079 — Samuel

After several controlled tests with temporal travel, I confirm what I already suspected: Markus and Lindsay are now tethered to me. Wherever I go — past or future — they follow, dragged along by proximity, not design. The storm altered me alone. The electrical anomaly marked my body in a way no protocol ever intended, and now their bodies and minds are caught in the wake of it. We are bound by consequence, not choice. We are entangled.

The IMC chip embedded in my brain is standard issue — a quiet safeguard carried by every citizen of my time. It was never meant to fracture reality. It exists to stabilize mental drift, operate communication, to manage trauma, to keep the mind tethered to the present during crisis. Yet when I cross timelines, it pulses rapidly, a sharp rhythm stuttering against my skull, as though struggling to interpret something it was never built to understand. I feel its rhythm like a second heartbeat, mechanical and confused, buried where certainty used to live.

Once Markus and Lindsay regain their strength, their emotions rise beyond my tolerance — fear, confusion, a pressure that hums through the air between us. They feel the distortion. But only I command it. Only I fall through it.

"Take us home! I need you to take us home!" Markus shouts, pacing across my living room. His voice trembles with the kind of panic I've forgotten people are capable of.

"My grandparents need me," Lindsay says, crying softly into a cup of water. She holds it with both hands, as if the act itself might keep her anchored.

They don't yet understand the gravity of their situation — or mine. I've seen versions of myself unravel when honesty comes too soon. This time, I lie.

"As soon as we fix what caused this, we can all go back," I say. My tone is calm — rehearsed calm. "Markus, sit down."

He obeys, though his leg shakes beneath the table. I can see his reflection in the glass wall — a young man trying to outstare despair.

"We fix this by destroying that comet in 2052, right?" Lindsay asks. Her voice cracks on the date, as if saying it makes the distance real. "How are we supposed to do something like that?"

"This comet is the reason everything's collapsing," I inform. "It pushed Earth slightly off orbit. That shift is why we're drowning in disasters — natural and man-made. In my time, the year you're standing in now, 2079, six months from today, the world burns."

Markus frowns. "Then why in the *hell* is my time already a nightmare?"

"The comet," I answer again, more softly. "It's to blame for everything."

He doesn't argue further. His silence is worse.

Lindsay wipes her eyes. "If Earth was pushed off orbit, that means we're drifting — losing protection from nearby planets, from everything out there. But how is that happening in 1999? Why does it affect us back then?"

"I'm asking the same thing," Jex says from the window, his tone even. "In 2052, the council debates whether to redirect the comet, but they vote against it when they learn it won't collide with us. If they'd known it would distort our magnetic field, maybe they would act differently."

"I'll make sure they do," I assure. "We leave in an hour."

Markus scoffs. "Or else what?"

"Or else I'll do it myself."

Jex looks at him curiously. "What is hell, anyhow?"

"Are you serious?" Markus replies.

"Jex," I say, cutting in, "in their time, people use religious terms. It's part of their culture."

"I see," Jex says. "Religion's illegal now — so are the words. Avoid using them."

Lindsay lowers her gaze. "Wow," she whispers.

"Sam," Jex says, "all your clothes were confiscated. I left one of my uniforms in the bathroom, mate."

"Thanks."

I change and catch my reflection — dark circles, faint bruises, eyes that seem older than I remember. The mirror flickers from delayed calibration. For a moment, it doesn't show me at all.

I decide to shower. Technically, I don't need to; the daily resets once made hygiene irrelevant. But now, with altered timelines and overlapping selves, it feels necessary — like a small declaration of control.

Under the water, I find myself thinking about the other me — the one who should be sleeping somewhere in this same city, unaware. Is he still there? Or do I overwrite him the moment I step across the boundary?

I finish quickly. Too many thoughts invite collapse.

When I step out, the air inside the apartment feels sterile. The hum of the air regulator is steady — too steady, almost sentient in its rhythm. I remember a day, years ago, when silence had meaning.

The anomaly that links Markus and Lindsay to me makes them passengers in this ordeal — pulled out of their 1999 and dropped into a century that no longer remembers them. I can't imagine their fear. But fear, like pain, dulls after repetition. I envy them for still feeling it sharply.

When I return, Markus meets me halfway. "Samuel," he says quietly, "can I save my aunt before we do anything else?"

"It's a no, Markus."

"Sam," Jex interjects, "even if you stop the comet, who's to say it'll fix their time — or yours?"

"We don't know," I say. "But we move forward. The council's looking for me, so we can't stay."

Lindsay studies me. "Why are they after you?"

"It's complicated."

"Maybe your government's behind this," Markus says.

"There are no governments anymore," I counter. "Just one."

Jex gives a short laugh. "That's one way to say it."

"It's the only way," I respond. "They call it the *Global Directorate*. One flag, one language set, one rulebook. It starts as a peace charter. Ends as a leash."

Lindsay looks between us. "So, there's no voting? No freedom?"

"Plenty of both," Jex says, smiling faintly. "You can vote for the same thing everyone else is already voting for. You can choose the shape of your cage."

Markus frowns. "That's not freedom."

"No," I respond. "It's comfort."

The word sits in the air like static. Lindsay rubs her arms as if she's felt a chill that isn't there.

She tries again. "What's it like — living there—living here I mean? In 2079?"

Jex answers before I can. "Quiet," he says. "Too quiet. The cities hum but no one talks above the noise. Air scrubbers keep the sky pale gray all year. Food comes in sealed packets; the taste depends on the memory you upload while eating. People don't die of hunger anymore, only disinterest."

"That's awful," Lindsay says.

He shrugs. "People call it peace."

I catch her gaze. "You'd call it lonely."

Markus leans forward, elbows on his knees. "In our time, it's loud — people yelling from cars, music blasting from every window. The air smells like gasoline and rain. Sometimes I hate it. Now it sounds like paradise."

"Paradise," Jex echoes softly, as if testing the word. "We erased that one too. It implies preference."

Markus looks at me. "How do you live without noise? Without… other people?"

"You learn to live inside your head," I say. "The Directorate calls it internal order. Everyone keeps their emotions calibrated to maintain productivity. Even love's been redefined as compatible frequencies with the help of our IMC's."

Lindsay shakes her head. "That's not living."

"It's surviving," I counter. "The two stop meaning the same thing a long time ago."

For a while none of us speak. The hum of the room fills the silence like a heartbeat that isn't ours.

Lindsay's voice comes small, but steady. "Can I ask about time travel?"

"You just did," Jex says.

She ignores him. "What's it like for you — when you time travel?" she asks, though she has already felt its teeth in her own mind.

I hesitate, then speak carefully. "It starts like electricity. A violent surge, sharp and blinding, as if something strikes the brain from the inside. Every nerve lights at once. Then it fades. The noise drains away. The body softens. Thought thins. And there is only quiet — a strange, suspended stillness, like falling into the space between seconds."

Markus rubs his face. "Neurological shock followed by dissociative drift," he mutters. "You're describing temporary sensory shutdown. It mirrors the early stages of clinical death."

"Maybe it resembles it," I say. "But it isn't death. You wake somewhere else, still whole, carrying every part of yourself — the weight, the memory, the ache of being human — only the world has shifted beneath your feet."

Lindsay looks at me carefully. "So what happens to us in 1999... now that we're here?"

"You're not there anymore," I say. "Not in any way that matters. You've been pulled forward, removed from your time and placed into mine. What remains behind isn't you — just the space you used to occupy."

She watches me, searching for certainty.

"I'm not completely sure," I add. "I don't fully understand what's happening to me yet. Or what it means for you."

A pause.

"You're being displaced. Taken out of your time and forced into a moment that does not belong to you. That is certain."

Jex leans back, watching them with clinical curiosity. "Do you remember the sensation?" he asks. "When he pulls you through?"

Markus nods slowly. "It's like every direction stretches at once. I can hear myself thinking in echoes. Then everything folds in, and there he is." He nods toward me. "And the world is wrong."

"It always is."

Lindsay wipes her eyes. "How do you stand it?"

"I don't," I reply. "I keep moving so I don't have to."

She hesitates, then smiles faintly. "That sounds like 1999."

Jex tilts his head. "Tell me about it — your time."

"It's messy," she says. "People still talk face to face. The air smells different. We still argue about small things — politics, music, weather — but it means something. We can touch each other without asking permission first."

Jex nods slowly. "Physical contact. Dangerous, but nostalgic."

"It's human," Markus says.

I look out the window where the skyline flickers under the haze. "Humanity doesn't vanish," I murmur. "It just learns how to hide."

No one replies. The moment stretches thin, like a wire waiting to break.

Before anyone can respond, the apartment lights dim. Then the door beeps.

"UNAUTHORIZED CLEARANCE. LOCAL AUTHORITIES ALERTED."

The shriek of the alarm fills the room.

Jex moves first. "They've found us!"

The door slides open and a sonar grenade rolls across the floor.

"Samuel!"

The blast hits like a wave of invisible glass. The air folds in on itself. My IMC chip screams in my skull — a static so deep it feels personal. I fall, open the interface, and hit reset. Reality convulses, pressure closing in from every direction. But because I haven't selected a date, the time-rift protocols stay dormant. The world fractures — controllable this time.

I force the system to stabilize, holding the moment still. The noise dies. The lights flicker. Smoke drifts through the doorway like a memory escaping.

"Roof access!" Jex shouts, dragging Markus toward the stairwell.

Lindsay covers her ears and follows, eyes wet from the blast. I stagger up, the IMC still pulsing behind my eyes, the calendar icon dark. Until I enter a time code manually, we are stuck in this timeline — no exits, no shortcuts.

We race up two flights. Emergency lights bleed red along the walls, strobing across our faces. The building shakes under another hit.

We burst onto the roof, the night sharp with cold air and neon haze. Below us, *Cyrius Avenue* glows with patrol lights — squads forming cordons at the intersections.

"There!" I point to the maintenance ladder bolted to the far ledge.

Markus goes first, then Lindsay. Her hands tremble as she climbs, but she doesn't stop.

Jex covers our retreat, firing two rounds into the stairwell. Sparks shower behind him. "They're locking down the east side!"

"Go!" I demand.

We drop into the alley behind the complex — rain-soaked concrete, air heavy with ozone. Neon light from *Cyrius Avenue* flickers off puddles like broken stars.

Jex hits the ground last, landing beside me. "They've sealed the west end," he says, catching his breath. "Drones are sweeping by twos now. You've got maybe an hour."

"That's more than enough."

He looks at me hard. "Your chip's unstable. You can't travel like this."

"I'm not phasing out yet," I reply. "Not until you're clear."

Markus and Lindsay lean against the wall, still shaking from the blast. Their faces are pale, half-lit by the sign of a shuttered café — *Orion District Diner.*

Jex holsters his weapon. "What's the plan?"

"You go to the cabin," I answer. "The one near the lake — where we fished that summer. Stay out of city range. Keep your name off the grid. Learn what you can about temporal interference, but don't dig deep. You were paramilitary — someone out there still owes you a favor."

He frowns. "They'll be looking for all of us."

"Not if you move first."

Jex hesitates, studying me. "And if they find the cabin?"

"Then they'll find an empty one."

He nods once, eyes flicking toward Markus and Lindsay. "You sure you can control it?"

"Only because I haven't selected a date," I say quietly. "The system's stable — for now."

He steps closer, gripping my shoulder. "Don't get lost in it."

I give a faint smile. "I won't."

Then he turns and disappears down the side street — coat flaring, footsteps fading into the hum of the city.

I wait until he's gone before facing the others.

Lindsay looks at me, her voice small. "What now?"

The chip interface pulses in my vision — the calendar screen reloading, blank and waiting.

"Now," I say, "we leave."

Markus straightens. "Where?"

"1999."

The air shifts. The ground ripples like a reflection about to break. I reach for them both, their hands cold against mine, and confirm the time-shift.

The city dissolves — light bending, sound collapsing — until only silence remains.

Then comes stillness. Weight leaves my body. The static in my skull fades like a dream breaking apart.

December 21st, 1999

I choose this year for a reason. Not sentiment. Not instinct. I need to know how far the tether stretches. If Markus and Lindsay can be pulled forward, then they can also be left behind. Disconnected. I have to see what time does to them

when the distance is this wide — whether the strain
weakens, or tightens into something unbreakable.

The air is different — thinner, cleaner. Dry grass brushes
against my palms, the earth cool beneath me. I scan the open
field where familiar structures have not yet risen, the skyline
reduced to emptiness and wind.

"Where are we?" Markus says, his voice carrying too far.
"Wait — this looks like home."

"Looks like home," Lindsay echoes, unsettled but certain.

"We're here to save your aunt," I tell them, already moving.
"That's why we're here."

Markus lingers. "If I'm here," he says slowly, "does that
mean there's no me in my room right now?"

I don't answer right away. I watch them instead — looking
for signs of fracture, of dislocation, of something beginning
to unravel.

"Exactly. You're here because this is where you are now," I
say, though I no longer believe it.

"What about Jex?" Lindsay asks.

"He'll manage."

"Markus, how long before it happens?"

"Two hours, maybe less."

"Then we move now."

"Samuel," Lindsay says softly. "You're not casting a shadow."

I freeze. The grass, the trees, the others — all have shadows. I don't.

A hum rises in my skull, faint and steady, like something whispering beneath the bone. Then it stops.

"Is that normal?" Markus asks.

"No," I say. "Not at all."

We move through streets that smell of fuel and iron. The air is thick — unfiltered, alive in its imperfection. For the first time, I realize how sterile the future truly is.

A dog barks as we pass a chain-link yard. It barks again, then goes silent — not because it recognizes me, but because it can't see me. Its eyes follow Lindsay instead, confused.

"This world remembers you," I tell her. "Not me."

Then the sky changes.
Red slides into violet. Violet thins into gold.

"This is what happens before the meteorites—" Markus begins.

"We keep moving," I say.

At the corner of Decanter and Morris Lane, he stops cold. "That's me," he whispers.

Across the street, his other self walks calmly by, a brown lunch bag in his hand, unaware, untouched.

Lindsay stares. "How is that even possible?"

"I don't know," I say. "My best guess? Time still needs him here. This year still requires him to exist to function as it should. So reality compensates." I watch the other Markus disappear down the road. "Either that... or this isn't your timeline at all."

He swallows but doesn't look away. "So I'm a duplicate."

"No," I murmur. "You're displaced. There's a difference."

"Move," I add.

We reach Carol just as she steps toward the train platform.

Markus rushes her, hands trembling, breath uneven. "Aunt Carol — you have to listen to me. You're not safe here. You need to leave, right now. Please."

She recoils, startled by his intensity. "Markus, what are you talking about? You're scaring people."

He gestures wildly toward the sky. "You don't understand. It's going to happen. You have to go. You have to go now."

Her face tightens. To her, he doesn't sound urgent. He sounds unstable.

"Step back," she warns, trying to steady him.

"Please," he insists, voice cracking. "Just trust me. Just move."

When he reaches for her arm, she slaps him — sharp, instinctive, defensive. A reflex born of fear, not anger.

"Don't touch me," she snaps. "You're acting like a lunatic."

"Look at the sky, Carol!" he shouts, desperate now. "Please!"

I step in before she can retreat further. "Go to the *Midnight Café*," I say calmly. "It's safer there."

She looks at me — searching, confused — caught between disbelief and some quiet instinct she doesn't yet understand. After a pause, she nods once and turns away.

We remain behind, watching her retreat.

I know what comes next. They don't.

The sky tears itself open.

Fire. Light. A sound so vast it feels like the heavens surrendering. The world folds under heat and ash.

Inside my mind, a clinical melody starts to play — one of the IMC's automated relaxation tracks — incongruously calm, as though the apocalypse has been assigned a soundtrack.

Lindsay screams for people to take cover, but the roar of splitting air consumes her voice. Above us, the sky convulses — streaks of fire tearing open the clouds, fragments blazing like falling suns. Shattered glass rings through the streets. Sirens wail and choke. The ground vibrates in shallow waves.

And inside my skull, impossibly, the IMC track continues — a slow, almost tender melody meant for anxious minds. Soft strings. Steady breath cues. It plays like a lullaby against the end of the world.

An hour seems to pass before silence returns.

"It's time," I say. "We move west."

"To Bloomfield?" Markus asks.

"Not yet. In your time, it's still a city. In mine, it's already a grave."

Lindsay grips his arm. "I think I'm in shock."

"I'm here," he says softly.

Behind us, Carol stumbles toward us through drifting ash.

"Markus!" she cries. "Please, come back. This isn't right."

He turns to her, torn. "Aunt Carol, you need to leave. Go home. Right now."

"It's not safe anywhere!" she pleads.

"It's safer than this," he insists, his voice raw with panic. "Please. Just go. Listen to me."

I meet her eyes. "This is only the beginning," I say calmly. "You have minutes, not time to argue."

"This is getting worse," I tell Markus, even as another meteor tears a white scar across the heavens. "She can't stay here. She needs to go home. It's safer inside. Shelter matters now."

She hesitates, terror and instinct warring in her face.

"Come home," she whispers one last time, her hand half-raised toward Markus.

"I can't," he says. "I have to help him. He saved you."

The words strike me harder than the thunder overhead.

Markus steps forward without hesitation and pulls his aunt into a tight embrace, his arms shaking as though the fear inside him has finally found somewhere to rest. For a brief moment she resists, confused, overwhelmed — then she softens against him, her breath hitching as she feels the urgency in his body. "Please, Aunt Carol," he murmurs, voice breaking. "You have to go inside. Right now." She studies his face, sees the terror he can no longer hide, and nods. Without another word, she turns and hurries toward the nearest building, disappearing through its doors just as another distant impact trembles through the ground. Markus watches until she is safely out of sight, his jaw clenched, the relief sharp and fleeting.

Another flash — closer now. The air hisses with heat.

"We won't make it," I murmur.

They don't ask what I mean. They just follow.

We run until the road gives way to open field. The grass ripples beneath our feet, glowing faintly with static discharge, every blade charged like a wire.

I stop.

"Here," I announce. "We travel from here."

"How do you know this won't drop us inside a wall?" Lindsay demands, breath sharp, eyes wide.

"I don't."

"Then why stop?" Markus presses.

The calm melody continues in my mind, serene and irreverent.

Because nowhere is safe, I think as I carefully select.

Before I can speak, the light crashes down upon us — blinding, absolute — and the world fractures again.

When I open my eyes, it is 2052.

The grass is cool against my back. The air thinner. Quieter.
As if the world itself speaks in a lower key.

Markus and Lindsay kneel beside me as the shimmer around
us fades and their forms reassert themselves — real again, or
close enough to believe.

"Thank you for saving my aunt," Markus says.

"You're welcome," I reply, though the words feel weightless.

And in that moment, I realize how easily the lie slips out —
how natural it has become —
like breathing in a world that no longer requires air.

Chapter Five
Year: 2052 — Markus

F irst thing Sam ever says that stays with me is that history isn't made by heroes — only by people who refuse to stop moving.

He says it like a confession more than a lesson, as if he already carries the weight of what comes next.
He tells us about the comet first — the story that shapes everything.

On May 12, 2052, the world governing body votes to stand idle. The decision is unanimous.
Dr. Alden Korr and his team at MASTRA present new

findings about the object they call *The Great Comet of '52*. Their calculations convince the council that the body will deflect itself — that no action is needed.

In school, I've learned that comets are mostly ice and dust — harmless until they aren't.
Korr's report says otherwise: the comet's core holds nickel and copper — a magnetic heart. That discovery changes everything.

When it passes by on May 19, it doesn't strike.
But it brushes Earth's magnetic field and tilts everything.

No one notices at first — the seasons stagger, the tides shift, the sky loses a certain color.
People call it a miracle. Sam calls it a sentence.

He blames Korr for the drift — says that one man's calculation has turned the planet into a slow-moving ruin.
From what I've seen of Sam — from what he's done for Lindsay and me — I have no reason to doubt him.

But sometimes, when he looks past us instead of at us, I'm not sure if I follow him out of loyalty or fear.

"Do you think he's all right?" Lindsay asks once, watching him sit beneath a tree and stare toward the horizon.

"He's exhausted," I say. I want to believe it is only that.

"You mean the lack of sleep," she says.

"How are you holding up, Linds?"

"A little in disbelief," she murmurs. "But I'll be okay." Then she grips my arm. "Marcus… something tells me Samuel isn't going to just talk to Dr. Korr."

"What do you mean?"

"I don't know. The way he spoke — the history lesson — I think if Korr refuses, he'll kill him."

"He's not going to kill anyone," I say too fast. "Wherever he goes, we go. He needs us."

"Or he kills us if we get in the way." Her hand slips off my arm. She is older than I am, and sharper when it comes to fear.

"He saved my aunt," I state. "We owe him that much."

"I don't trust him," she whispers.

"We have no choice. You trust me, though, right?"

"I trust you." Her face softens. "I trust you'll do the right thing."

I promise I will, though the words feel smaller each time I say them.

Sam explains the world's mistakes like a man tracing old wounds.

In 2035, *Magnetic Aero* builds the first atmospheric field engines — experimental crafts meant to imitate magnetism through plasma thrust, not ride it.

They call it a "simulation of the earth's magnetic equilibrium," but it is guesswork built on hope and electricity.

Two years later, *Astra Agency* takes over orbital research, promising a cleaner kind of propulsion — "progress without combustion."

By 2052, the two merge and become MASTRA — the global command of every sky-bound system: aircraft, satellites, weather control.

After the comet passes, their guesswork finally meets the real thing. The planet's magnetism changes — and they adapt before anyone else.

Sam says they don't just study the shift; they weaponize it. He says MASTRA's emblem — two crossing magnetic fields — is meant to symbolize unity.

"But all symbols rot," he tells us. "Give them time."

He speaks about MASTRA as if it is fate itself, not an organization.

"They called it progress," he says once, "but it was ownership — of the sky, of the data, of us."

Later, I see that same emblem stitched on the sleeves of our stolen uniforms.

"If he refuses," Sam says, "we leave him no choice."

"You'd kill him," I say before I can stop myself.

Sam doesn't deny it. "If it saves everyone else."

"That's not saving," Lindsay says sharply. "That's rewriting one disaster with another."

"Dr. Korr made this mess," Sam replies, voice low and deliberate — not angry, not pleading.
"He's the reason we're standing here at all."

"And killing him fixes that?" I ask. "What if you're wrong? What if we just tear the same hole twice?"

He stares at me — not at my face, but through it, like he is looking at a version of me that has already agreed.

For a long moment, none of us speak. The wind comes through the grass like static.

"We find another way," I say finally.

Lindsay steps closer to him. "You said we were in this together. Then listen to us."

Sam's jaw tightens. The silence stretches. Then he looks down, the fight draining from his eyes.

"Fine," he says. "Plan B."

He does not explain himself — not then.

But later, when we have gone quiet and the night pulls thin over the land, I see him kneeling by the edge of the fire, drawing into the dirt with a careful, deliberate hand. He moves as if he is remembering something rather than inventing it. Circles, angles, a strange symmetry that makes no sense to me and yet feels disturbingly precise.

I do not interrupt. There is something solemn in the way he works, as though the ground itself has already agreed to receive what he is giving it.

I realize then that he has not lost his nerve, only redirected it. What I mistook for hesitation is something else entirely — a slow recalibration, a quiet shifting of compass and marrow. He has not abandoned the path. He has revised where it leads.

It is not surrender. It is a measured deviation.
And somehow, that unsettles me more. The fire dims. The soil remembers. And he continues, long after the world around us has chosen silence.

One Year Later — Same Year: 2052

We live the same day for a year.

Every attempt to infiltrate the MASTRA compound fails. Wrong codes. Locked gates. A guard turning at the wrong second.

Each time we are seconds from capture, Sam triggers the reset — and the morning begins again.

At first, it is bearable.
We joke, we keep notes — some that guide us, others that

fade into irrelevance — but we write them all the same, as if remembrance itself might one day outlast the repetition.

Lindsay keeps a mental list of what works and what doesn't — she calls it "our invisible diary."

By the fourth week, we are professionals at failure.

We learn that a left-handed guard named Weaver drops his coffee at 06:13 if someone leaves a mug too close to the corner of the break-room table.
That spill buys us thirteen seconds to cross Hall 'C' unseen.

We learn that the biometric door on Level 2 misreads a badge if you swipe twice too quickly.

We learn that humming under your breath keeps the voice scanners from catching nervous tremors.

Lindsay starts naming the loops: *The Coffee Spill. The Lock Jam. The Badge Lag.*
She says it makes them sound like chapters instead of punishments.

Sam tracks the resets like scripture.
He mutters reminders before each attempt — "Don't forget to breathe before the third door," or "Shift your weight before the guard looks left."

The smallest mistake means starting over.
The air bends, and suddenly it is dawn — same light, same dew, same birdsong cut by engines.

At first, it is beautiful. Then it is torture.

Sam grows quieter. He begins watching us the way scientists watch a flame — to see what burns first.

He trains us like soldiers: how to walk, how to salute, how to breathe in rhythm with the cameras.
At first, it feels like survival. Later, it feels like obedience.

Ever since the day we see that soldier of light dissolve into the air, every one of Sam's time-rift pulls us with him.
He says it is "IMC interference," a glitch in the circuit of his brain.

I don't believe him. It feels like something else — like the world itself has decided we belong to his mistake. By the twelfth month, I can't tell where one attempt ends and another begins. The days blur into the hum of power lines and the ache of doing the same thing wrong in a thousand different ways. Only Sam seems unchanged — locked inside his conviction that if he can't reason with Dr. Korr, he'll fix the world himself.

Sam gives us a list.
He says it is everything he has learned over the year — a choreography of small lies that might add up to an honest chance.

He teaches it to us like prayers.
I still remember it word for word.

1. **Suit the part.**
   Wear the uniform before you get close. Let the
   jacket be the first lie the cameras accept.
   Smell the fabric to convince your skin: soap,
   sanctioned detergent, nothing personal.
   A uniform makes a stranger look like he belongs.

2. **Move in patterns.**
   Keep your gait even. Don't hurry, don't pause to
   stare. Cameras are trained on people who break
   rhythm. Breathe with a clock in your chest and let
   everything else fall in line.

3. **Eye-contact economy.**
   Meet a guard's gaze for three beats, then look away
   politely. Too long and you're a question. Too short
   and you're a ghost.
   Sam times it with a hand under his breath; we
   practice the count until our eyes sting.

4. **Small talk, minimal.**
   A nod, a weather remark, something that ends.
   Conversation that lingers invites inspection. Keep
   phrases mechanical and soft — the sort of lines
   officers use on a long morning.

5. **Badge choreography.**
   Swipe with confidence, not speed. Present the badge
   as proof, not explanation.
   If a reader blinks, smile like you're answering a joke
   you already know the punchline to.

6. **Mirror the room.**
   If everyone carries a tablet, carry one. If people
   glance at a screen, glance too.
   The simplest mimicry is the best camouflage.

7. **Control the noise.**
   Don't speak over alarms; let the building's soundscape own you.
   Use silence to your advantage — make it look like you're listening to an order.

8. **Exit strategy rehearse.**
   Know three ways out. If the door you plan fails, have the second and third memorized down to the scuff marks and the emergency latch.
   Never assume one route is enough.

9. **Hold the line.**
   If something goes wrong, keep moving. Hesitation is contagious.
   A team that hesitates breaks faster than anything else.

10. **If discovered, look like procedure.**
    If a guard approaches, raise your palms, go procedural — apologize, state compliance, and redirect.
    Fear shows in flinch; practice a calm that reads as routine.

We run the list until it sticks in our teeth.
Sam's voice reduces each item to a single image — a badge that glows green, the three-beat look, the rhythm of a walk that is not hurried.

He tells us which corridors are loud and which are watched, which consoles will accept manual input, and which will lock the room down.

He teaches us how to pause with a laugh that means nothing, how to let a guard believe he has already seen you before.

The Infiltration — May 18, 2052

By the time the real day arrives, it feels rehearsed.

We wear MASTRA uniforms — navy, the insignia in silver thread over the chest.
Sam's arm is wrapped in gauze from a wound he carries across resets; he says the pain helps him stay alert.

The corridors smell of ozone and sterilized metal.
Every step echoes too loudly; every camera blinks like a silent accusation.

Sam walks first, posture steady, face unreadable beneath the navy brim.
"Remember," he whispers, "machines see patterns, not nerves. Breathe like you belong."

Lindsay's badge flickers green. The security door sighs open.

I feel the hum of the compound through the soles of my boots — like the building is aware of us.

The launch room is cathedral-bright, white so severe it feels ceremonial, as though even the machines understand the gravity of what we are about to do. Light spills from every surface — panels, glass, polished steel — and the air hums with restrained electricity, a chorus of systems whispering to one another in coded reverence.

The walls breathe data. Vectors crawl across towering screens: orbital paths, rotational velocity, magnetospheric

distortions. The comet looms there in cold, exquisite clarity
— not the streak of fire one imagines, but a beautiful,
indifferent mass, mottled with ancient scars, its tail
unraveling like a wound in space.

Sam is already moving.
His fingers blur across the console, a choreography of
desperation and precision, keys responding to him like
something trained. Every input feels like trespass. Every
second borrowed.

"One wrong line," he mutters, "and they'll see us."

He doesn't glance back. He doesn't need to.

"Missile T-12," he says. "Manual override."

I swallow. The screen in front of me fractures into layered
telemetry — guidance arrays coming online, the satellite link
initializing. MASTRA's own orbital sentinel pivots above us,
sleek and silent, its sensors awakening to serve a weapon not
meant to exist.

"Target locked," I say, though my voice betrays me. There is
no ceremony left in its sound.

The weapon itself is almost modest. Not the hulking terror
of old wars, but something refined, concentrated —
precision given form. A narrow spine of alloy and plasma
core, its warhead condensed, accelerated beyond anything
built for atmosphere. Velocity numbers scroll past
comprehension. Mach-figures turn meaningless. It is speed
weaponized into inevitability.

The satellite blinks green — guidance confirmed.
Artificial intelligence fused with ancient trajectory.
MASTRA's eye turned against the sky.

The sirens hush.

Not silence, but a reverent pause.
A mechanical prayer.

Then the ground answers.

The launch erupts — not an explosion, but a violent
ascension. White fire claws upward through reinforced glass,
through cloud, through the illusion that the sky was ever
protective. Cameras chase it in brutal clarity — a needle of
light piercing infinite dark, shrinking as it conquers altitude.

We say nothing.

The comet grows on the monitors, slow and merciless, its
surface rotating like something alive, and for the briefest,
most dangerous moment, I believe.

Light blossoms.
A violent starburst against the void.

"Direct hit," Lindsay breathes.

Color fractures across the comet's face — iridescent
shockwaves blooming like bruises across ancient stone. The
room almost exhales.

Then the fracture closes.

The comet shudders — and corrects.

Its trajectory stabilizes, cruelly unbothered.
A god shrugging off a pinprick.

"Only a scratch," Sam murmurs.

But his voice… it no longer carries belief. Only knowledge.
The kind that settles in the bones and refuses warmth
forever.

The monitors flood red. Angles recalculated. Impact
probabilities rewritten in merciless percentages. The satellite
continues tracking — loyal, obedient, oblivious.

And in the crimson wash of emergency light, I see it in his
face.

Not fear.
Not rage.

Recognition.

Gunfire cracks behind us.
The spell collapses.

Glass screams. Sparks scatter.
And the room that once felt like a sanctuary becomes what it
always was — a chamber of borrowed time.

Sam doesn't flinch when the bullet tears through his
shoulder; he just stares at the screen as if he can *will* the
comet apart by looking.

"Move!" he shouts.

We run through smoke, the floors trembling under the klaxons. The corridors blur.

The world folds into sound. It feels like every failed attempt has been preparing us for this exact failure.

Outside, the horizon is red. Sirens wail through the haze.

Sam presses his hand to his wound, his voice faint but steady.
"So much control over time," he says, "but absolutely no control of the outcomes."

He looks up as if he can still bend fate back with his will alone.

Lindsay reaches for him, but he pulls away. His eyes have gone glassy — not from pain, but from knowing he can't undo this one.

"We failed again," she says.

"No," Sam murmurs. "Not yet."

He takes out his phone, his blood leaving small red circles across the screen.

"Sam, —" I begin, but before the words can reach him, the tether ignites.

The air bends.
My vision splits into three colors.
Lindsay's hand finds mine.

Then everything is light.

The sky folds. The world vanishes.

For an instant, I see the missile's trail curve across the horizon like a scar that refuses to heal.

Then silence.

We are gone — dragged through the fold with him.
Bound to Sam — not by choice or mercy, but by whatever the light decides.

A comet breathes past us,
silver silence scars the sky,
our shadows whisper home.

MASTRA

Chapter SIX
Year: 2079 — Markus

W hen the light clears, we are back in 2079;
Sam's present.
The same skyline. The same humming air.
The same failure.

Sam stands in the middle of the apartment, silent.
Lindsay sits on the floor, head in her hands.
The city below looks alive and dead at once —
the magnetic haze bending over the streets like heat.

For a moment none of us speak.
Then Sam says, "We finish what we started."

"You mean Korr," Lindsay whispers.

He doesn't answer. He doesn't have to.
The sound of his voice makes the room feel smaller, like air sealing around us.
I can tell he's already decided what comes next.

He leads us into the city's lower district, where the towers end and the old streets begin.
The neon flickers unevenly down here, where the fields of magnetism don't reach.
No one looks at us. No one cares who walks by anymore.
Perhaps my anxiety subsides.

We follow him through rows of antique shops — places that smell of oil, rust, and damp wood.
Their signs hang crooked in languages no one uses.

Sam stops at one window. Dusty glass.
Inside: brass clocks, pocket lighters, and, behind the counter, a small display of firearms that look a century out of place; especially in Sam's world.

He steps inside.
We wait.
A minute later, he comes back out, his coat folded slightly at the side where the shape of a revolver presses against it.

He hasn't paid.
The owner says nothing, only stares through him — as if knowing it won't matter.

"Sam," I say. "You can't just—"

He doesn't reply.

He takes out his phone, thumb over the screen.
Its surface catches the dull orange light.
The calendar glows.
One tap.
A pulse of blue.

His other hand brushes the spot behind his ear — where the
IMC chip is inserted into his brain, buried in him like a
second heart. The standard.

The air bends.
Then it breaks.

We land in a flash of bright white — a conference hall filled
with glass and steel.

Year — 2052

The air smells new, as if the century itself has just been
polished clean of hesitation. The city unfolds around us in
glass and pale metal, cleaner than memory, sharper than
anything we left behind. Vehicles glide past in disciplined
silence, guided by rails of invisible precision.

Sam does not hesitate.

A sleek transport idles at the curb — driver distracted,
screen glowing soft and blue — and Sam moves with a
swiftness that feels almost cruel. The door jerks open. A
startled shout. A confused protest swallowed by the flow of
time.

"Out," Sam says, voice low, final.

The man stumbles back in shock as Sam slides into the driver's seat.
"Now," he snaps.

Lindsay and I climb in without argument.

The car hums alive beneath us, responding to his touch like a nervous animal recognizing its master.

Coordinates spill across the dashboard — government zone, research district, elevated access only. Dr. Korr's name flashes in red among scheduled engagements.

"Lecture hall," Sam mutters. "He's speaking today."

Of course he is.

The road stretches like a promise we intend to break. Towers rise, sleek and tensile, the world of tomorrow breathing calmly while we tear through it in borrowed seconds. The horizon burns gold with artificial sun-strips. Screens pulse with optimistic slogans about unity, preservation, cosmic harmony.

None of it belongs to us.

Lindsay watches the city pass with a quiet unease.
"You're sure it's him?" she asks.

Sam doesn't look away.
"There's only one man who says the comet will save us."

Silence settles — thick, knowing.

The transport slows near an immense structure of glass and reinforced white steel. MASTRA insignia gleams along its exterior like a promise engraved into stone.

People gather, composed and curious, faces full of belief.

We step out into their certainty like trespassers in a cathedral.

Inside, light floods the auditorium, cascading over rows of expectant bodies. The air vibrates with reverence. Anticipation.

And there he is.

Dr. Alden Korr stands at the podium, composed, assured — his hands resting calmly as though the future itself has granted him permission to speak.

Projected behind him, glowing in pristine clarity:

"The Great Comet: Our Salvation, Not Our Doom."

Sam's jaw tightens beside me.
I feel Lindsay's breath grow shallow.

We have crossed time not into chaos — but into conviction.

And for the first time, I realize the true danger may not be the man himself, but how convincingly the world believes him.

He is older than I expect.
Calm, exacting. The kind of man who thinks equations are
moral truths.

Sam raises the revolver before Lindsay or I can react.

"Sam, no—" I shout, but the sound drowns in the echo of
the gunshot.

Korr's eyes widen.
He falls without a word.
The sound of his body hitting the floor is softer than I
imagine.

Sam lowers the gun, his voice steady, distant:
"You can't fix rot. You can only stop the spread."

Lindsay screams. I freeze.
For a moment, time itself seems to hold its breath.

Then Sam presses his thumb to the calendar again.
The world folds.

We are back where we started.
The same skyline.
The same orbit patterns above the city. The same
magnificent future of magnetism.
Nothing has changed.

Sam's Present Year — 2079

Lindsay's voice cracks. "You killed him for nothing."

Sam doesn't respond. He unlocks his archives instead, the glow from the screen bleeding across his hands.

I watch his eyes dart between lines of text, static flashing across the glass.
Then he stops scrolling.

"They knew," he whispers. "The council. MASTRA. They knew what would happen."

He looks sick. "They wanted the comet close — to harvest it. They thought they could control the field drift."

Lindsay turns away.

"So everything—" she begins, "—everything you've done, all of it—"

Sam interrupts quietly.
"They underestimated the catastrophe."

For the first time, I see him look unsure.
Not angry — hollow.
Like belief itself is dissolving.

Lindsay says softly, "Then don't make the same mistake. Don't meet her."

Sam freezes. "Who?"

"Juliette."

He doesn't answer right away. The name hits him like something remembered in a dream — fragile, half-believed.

His jaw tightens, a flicker of pain crossing his face before he buries it.

For a moment, he looks like someone caught between two versions of himself — the man who has already lost her, and the man who hasn't met her yet.

He closes his eyes. His breathing steadies, too even, too practiced. When he opens them again, he looks almost human — not the commander or the scientist, but the boy who still thinks time can be reasoned with.

"She's the reason all of this started," he says quietly. "If I stay away from her, maybe it ends."

"Or maybe it never begins," Lindsay says.

The silence that follows is heavy — not argument, not peace, just the sound of three people realizing that even love has become another variable in Sam's experiment with time.

The time transition is smoother this time.
A quiet street.
Air still clean enough to breathe without noticing static waves.

Year — 2079 — A few months back.

A café with a wooden sign that reads *Solar Bean*.

Juliette sits outside, laughing with someone unseen — sunlight moving across her hair like a secret.

Sam doesn't move closer.
He only stands there, watching.
Not hiding, but not intruding either.

It is strange, seeing him still. For once he isn't calculating or planning — he isn't the man who can twist time like a thread around his fingers. He is just someone who remembers what it feels like to stand in daylight and let it touch him.

I've never realized how quiet he can be when he isn't in command. The way he breathes — slow, measured — feels like he is teaching himself to exist again, one second at a time.

He looks… leveled. Still in a way I haven't thought possible. The edges of him soften, the anger dormant.

I understand then — the silence isn't guilt. It is restraint. The kind of stillness that comes after too much movement.

"Why doesn't she see you?" Lindsay asks.

"Different laws," Sam says. His voice is low, even. "Different realities, different limits. Some worlds aren't meant to recognize what doesn't belong."

He gives a faint, almost tired smile — the kind that doesn't reach his eyes.

"I'm fortunate to land in this one," he says quietly. "A reality where I can't mess up by talking to her right now."

For a second, the world feels balanced — as if the universe itself is giving him mercy by setting the distance.

He watches Juliette for another moment, long enough to memorize the shape of her in the sun. Then he turns away.

"Let's go," he says.

I hesitate. The street around us feels almost sacred — sunlight hanging like dust caught in still water. For a moment, I don't want to move. Maybe Lindsay doesn't either. There is something final in the way Sam turns away from Juliette, like a man closing a door he's been trapped behind for years.

I wonder if he really believes what he says — that staying away can stop it all. Maybe he does. Maybe it is easier to think the universe can be negotiated with, that time can be persuaded by remorse. But standing there, I see what it really is: surrender dressed as logic.

Every version of him we've met has been chasing a fix, rewriting the same sin in cleaner ink. And here, for the first time, he looks tired enough to let the ink dry.

When he walks ahead, Lindsay follows without a word. I take one last look at the café, at the woman who unknowingly haunts a thousand timelines, and then at the man who keeps trying to save her by losing her.

I did not know then that mercy could so closely resemble madness.
The air begins to hum.

Year — 1999

The rift is rougher this time — like the world resists being rewritten again. The air tears, then mends. We hit the ground hard — grass and dust beneath our hands.

I blink, squinting at the sunlight. The sky flickers in faint bands of color — blue, green, then red — as if light itself is glitching.

Sam stands first, breathing deeply, his eyes scanning the horizon. There is no city skyline, no magnetic haze, no hum of future air — just a quiet field on the edge of a small town. A car rattles past on a cracked road, its radio spilling static and a voice singing something half-forgotten.

He doesn't check his device, doesn't even look back at the sky.

"We're not going forward," Lindsay says. "You're not going to see if she—"

"No," Sam interrupts. "I've seen enough of endings. I want to try living somewhere that still has beginnings."

The words hang there, soft but final in 1999.

As we walk toward the town, I notice a faded bumper sticker on a car parked by a diner: "Man on the Moon – '69."

"Lindsay," I say, pointing to it, "you remember the moon landing in '69?"

She smiles faintly. "Of course. Armstrong, 'one small step,' and all that."

I pause. "That's strange. I learned it happened in '71."

She stops walking. The air between us seems to thin.

"What are you saying?"

"I think," I say quietly, "we're not from the same world."

She looks at Sam, but he says nothing — just keeps staring toward the town, as if memorizing its vintage silence.

Different years. Different truths. Same mistake.

For the first time, I realize we haven't escaped the loop — we've only changed its shape. The girl I've grown attached to doesn't belong where I'm from. She belongs in a place that might not even exist in my version of reality.

I turn to Sam. "Do you think she could be found in my world?"

He looks at me, trying to understand.

"I mean," I say, "the version of 1999 I came from — if she's there too, would she remember me?"

Sam's face softens. "I don't know," he says quietly. "It seems that you and Lindsay aren't from the same strand. The timelines forked long before either of you met. Even if she exists in your world... she wouldn't know you. Not the way you remember her."

He pauses, eyes drifting toward the horizon. "I've spent so much time crossing worlds that all look like mine. After a while, you stop trusting what's real — even your own timeline."

The words sit between us like dust settling after an explosion — soft, but final.

That's when I understand — the fracture isn't just in time. It is in us. Each of us from a slightly different cut of the same story, stitched together by desperation.

The silence stretches until Lindsay breaks it.

She screams, clutching her head, the sound raw and human in a world that is anything but. "Stop!" she shouts. "Just stop moving us!"

Sam steps forward, but she pulls away.

He doesn't move again.

He is the tether — the quiet gravity that keeps us from drifting. Through him, Lindsay and I stay connected, two echoes sharing the same fault line.

Lindsay walks away, sitting on a patch of grass near a tree. Her shoulders tremble, her face turned from the wind. She needs distance — space to breathe, or maybe to break. He looks at me for a long moment — then says quietly, "You like her, don't you?"

I freeze. "What?"

"Lindsay," he clarifies. "You care about her. For real."

I want to deny it, but the words won't come. "I... I don't know. We've been through too much. A year of fixing time, trying to stop the world from tearing itself apart. You start to... care."

Sam nods, a faint ghost of a smile crossing his face. "Good."

He reaches into his cargo pocket, rummaging through the folds until he pulls out two metallic rings, dull silver with faint circuitry etched into their bands.

"These belonged to Jex Titor," Sam says, turning them in his palm. "My old roommate. He bought them years ago for someone — it didn't work out. I found them in my pocket the day we prepped the warhead for the comet."

He hands them to me. The rings are warm, almost pulsing with a quiet hum.

"Mag-C rings," he says. "They resonate when they're close. The magnetic fields pull toward each other, no matter what's between them. They're not just tech — they're connection. Even when things drift."

I stare down at them, unsure. "Why give them to me?"

He looks toward Lindsay. "Because she needs something to hold onto. And maybe you do too."

I take the rings, feeling their subtle vibration in my hand. When I walk over, Lindsay doesn't look up at first.

"I don't belong anywhere," she says, voice breaking. "Every time I think I do, it comes undone."

I crouch beside her, holding out one of the rings. "You belong here. Right now. With me."

She blinks at it, then at me. "What is this?"

"A promise," I say quietly. "A friendship ring. Or whatever this is supposed to be."

She hesitates — then smiles, small but real. "You're terrible at timing, Markus."

"Yeah," I say. "But at least I'm consistent."

She takes the ring and slides it onto her finger. The two Mag-C bands pulse once, faint blue light tracing the grooves like veins of electricity finding each other across a gap.

Her tears slow, and the tremor in her hands fades. The wind eases.

It feels like two storms finding the same calm, if only for a heartbeat.

For the first time in forever, the world isn't falling apart — it is simply still. When the wind finally settles, Lindsay looks up, wiping her face with the back of her hand. "What now?" she asks.

"Carol," I say. "We find her."

Sam turns his head slightly, the muscles in his jaw tightening. "Your aunt?"

"She's here. Or should be," I say. "You said she survives this timeline."

Sam doesn't answer right away. He looks off toward the horizon, the fields fading into the dim orange of a setting sun. Something in his silence unsettles me.

"You don't think she's alive," I add.

He meets my eyes, expression unreadable. "I think time remembers what it wants. The rest—"

"Don't," I snap. "You promised she'd make it."

Lindsay touches my shoulder. "Maybe he's just—"

"I said she's alive," I cut her off. My voice comes out sharper than I mean. "She's the only family I've got left. The only thing that still connects me to before."

Sam slips his hands into his coat pockets. "Then let's go find her."

He says it flatly — not with conviction, but with the tone of someone preparing for a truth they don't want confirmed.

The three of us walk toward the town's edge. The streets grow quieter the farther we go, like the world itself is holding its breath. Neon signs blink out one by one until only the faint hum of the Mag-C rings breaks the silence.

Even before we reach the address, I can feel something wrong — the static in the air, the way Sam's pace slows. When we stop in front of the small brick complex, my chest feels hollow.

When things finally still, I search for my aunt — the woman Sam swears will survive.

She hasn't.

The reports say she dies the same day as before.

I find Sam staring out at the night sky, his phone glowing faintly in his hand.

"You lied," I say.

He doesn't turn around.

"I needed you to believe," he says.
"Belief gets you further than truth."

Something in me breaks.

I hit him.
The sound is raw — skin against bone.

He stumbles but doesn't fight back.

I swing again.

He catches my arm, his grip firm but not cruel.

"You're angry at the wrong thing," he says.

"I trusted you!"

"I know."

My next blow hits his wounded shoulder — the same one from the missile base.

He grimaces, drops his phone.

It hits the ground.
The screen splinters, a thin crack running through it — not shattered, just broken enough.

The glow bleeds unevenly now, like a pulse skipping beats.

A low hum seeps out of it; faint, mechanical, and wrong.

Lindsay doesn't move at first — just stares at the humming device, her voice trembling but fierce.

"Sam, what did you just do?" she demands. Then her eyes shift to me. "What did *you* do?"

He stares at the fractured glass.
His reflection splits into two halves, blinking out of sync.

The hum deepens, resonating in the air, in the grass, in our bones.

Time doesn't shatter all at once.
It starts with a single crack —
in glass, in faith, in the idea that any of this could still be fixed.

Chapter Seven

Year: 1999 — Markus

T he phone is cracked. It lies face-down on the pavement, blue light bleeding faintly from the fracture. None of us speak at first.

"You lied to me," I snap. "About Carol. About everything."

Sam doesn't look up. His breathing is uneven, his shoulders tight.

"I need you to believe," he says quietly. "Belief gets you further than truth."

"Further?" I step closer. "You call that progress? You used us."

"I do what I have to."

"Then what is any of it for?" I cut in. "She's still dead, Samuel. Nothing changes."

He finally raises his head. There is no anger in his face — just exhaustion and a thin sheen of sweat forming at his hairline.

"Markus," he says, voice low, almost pleading, "you don't understand what it's like—"

"No," I cut him off. "You don't understand what it's like being dragged through time chasing someone else's mistake."

"Stop," Lindsay says softly, but neither of us listens.

Sam opens his mouth to speak again, then stops. His hand trembles slightly at his side. He blinks hard, as if trying to focus.

"Sam?" Lindsay says.

He sways. The color drains from his face.

"Sam, what's wrong?"

"I... don't..." he starts, but the words break apart mid-sentence. His eyes unfocus, then roll back.

Light flickers faintly beneath his skin — a pale blue tracing along the veins at his temple and down the side of his neck, pulsing in uneven rhythm.

"Sam!" Lindsay yells.

He collapses, slamming into a row of trash cans. The sound echoes down the alley.

I freeze. My anger vanishes in an instant.

Lindsay drops beside him, pressing a hand to his forehead. "He's burning up," she says. "God, he's overheating."

The light under his skin flares again, sharp enough to make the veins stand out like lit wires. His breathing comes shallow and fast.

"What's happening to him?" I ask.

"It's his arm," she says, pulling back his sleeve. The wound from the missile base is swollen, red, the skin around it streaked and raw. "It's infected — badly. And the chip's reacting to it."

"The chip?"

She nods, panicked. "The IMC monitors internal vitals, remember? If it detects infection, it tries to regulate body temperature and blood chemistry — but it must not be designed for infected puncture wounds. It's overloading, sending constant corrections through his nervous system."

Her eyes catch something on the ground — the phone. The crack in its screen pulses in sync with the light beneath Sam's skin.

She picks it up carefully. "It's still connected," she whispers. "The feedback's looping between him and the device. It's burning him from the inside out."

Sam twitches once, then goes completely still.

"Is he—"

"He's alive," Lindsay says, her hand still on his chest. "Barely." She looks at me, desperate. "We have to move him. *Now.*"

We drag him deeper into the alley — his weight feels heavier than human. I can feel the tremors through him; every few seconds his body jerks again, like static running through bone.

"Then we need to get him somewhere safe," I say.

Lindsay's eyes dart toward the street. "There!"

A delivery truck idles at the curb, engine still running, driver nowhere in sight.

"You're not serious,"

She turns to me, eyes blazing. "We don't have time to be moral, Markus."

We lift Sam into the back of the truck and lay him across the floor among cardboard crates labeled *Garden Goods*. I slide into the passenger seat while Lindsay climbs behind the wheel.

The engine growls. She shifts gears and peels into the street.

The city blurs around us — rain, sirens, red lights reflected in puddles. Somewhere, an alarm has gone off. Maybe ours.

Sam's breathing grows ragged. The blue light beneath his skin pulses faster now, crawling up his neck like veins of lightning.

"We need medicine," Lindsay says. "Something for the infection."

"There's a pharmacy ahead," I tell her.

She slams the brakes, turning hard into a side street. I jump out before the truck even stops moving. The glass door of the pharmacy jingles as I push inside. A clerk behind the counter barely looks up.

"Where's your penicillin?" I ask.

He squints. "Prescription only."

I vault the counter.

"Hey—!"

But I'm already digging through drawers. I find a small vial and a hypodermic needle sealed in plastic. The alarm trips the moment I land back over the counter. On instinct, I grab a first-aid kit from the wall as I run for the door — bandages, gauze, antiseptic, whatever I can carry.

"Markus!" Lindsay yells from outside.

"I've got it!"

I sprint out, sirens already wailing in the distance. Lindsay guns the engine. We speed through downtown streets, tires skidding across wet asphalt.

Two police cars catch our tail, lights flashing like broken stars.

"Hold on," Lindsay says.

She cuts hard through an intersection, narrowly missing a sedan. Horns blare. The truck's rear tires fishtail through a red light.

"Drive faster," I say.

"I'm already doing that," she snaps.

"You're going to kill us."

"Better than letting them catch us."

"Maybe we should stop," I say. "Maybe we tell them—"

"Tell them what?" she shouts over the wind. "That our friend's glowing and dying from a government chip that doesn't exist?"

I don't answer.

The cruiser behind us surges closer, tires hissing over wet pavement. The rain makes everything slick — the streetlamps a blur of gold and orange. A trash bin topples as we tear past, scattering garbage into the air like confetti.

Lindsay grips the wheel tighter. "You trust me?"

"Right now?"

"Just say yes."

"Yes!"

"Then hang on!"

She yanks the wheel right, cutting down a narrow service road between two shuttered buildings. The truck barely fits — metal scraping brick. Sparks fly. The police car overshoots the turn, skidding out and smashing into a parked van.

Lindsay doesn't slow down.

"Holy—" I can't finish.

The road opens into the industrial district, long rows of warehouses half-drowned in fog. The city lights behind us fade to a dull, trembling glow.

"You did it," I say.

"Got lucky," she mutters, eyes still on the road.

Rain drums harder against the windshield. Sam groans in the back, his skin faintly glowing with that pale, unnatural light.

Neither of us speaks. The adrenaline fades, leaving only the quiet thrum of the tires and the storm.

"Where are we going?" I ask.

"Port Mason," she says. "My world. My time. If we keep heading north, we'll reach *Eldridge Valley* — it's quiet there. No one looks for anyone in the valley."

The road narrows as it climbs into the hills. The glow of the city behind us sinks beneath the treeline. Power lines sway overhead, humming faintly in the wind — an eerie, low vibration neither of us mentions.

At the edge of the ridge, Lindsay kills the headlights. The world goes black except for the faint pulse of blue from Sam's body. The rain slows to a mist.

"We're here," she whispers.

We lift Sam from the truck and lay him in the grass. His skin is hot, fever burning under the surface. I open the box, unfold the tiny instruction slip, and stare at the words.

"Half of this isn't even English," I mutter.

"Just read," she says. Her hands shake as she preps the syringe.

I watch her draw the penicillin, tap the air bubbles free. "You ever done this before?"

"Once," she says. "When I was a kid. I was sick for weeks. My mom—" She stops herself. "It worked."

She steadies the needle against Sam's arm. I place a hand on her shoulder, keeping her from shaking. The injection goes in clean.

Then we wait.

The wind moves softly through the trees. Somewhere far below, water whispers against rock.

Lindsay sits beside me, knees drawn to her chest. "Do you think he really loved her?"

"Juliette?" I ask.

She nods.

"Yeah. I think he does. Enough to break the world for her."

She smiles faintly. "That's kind of terrifying."

"I know."

"You ever felt that way?"

I think of her — the way her platinum hair catches the last line of sun, the steadiness in her voice when everything else trembles and her gentle porcelain skin. "Maybe," I say.

She looks at me then, not smiling this time. "Maybe?"

"Fine," I say. "Yes."

Lindsay leans back against the truck, the night wind
threading through her hair. She turns her hand over, the
faint blue pulse from the ring casting small flickers across her
skin.

"Funny," she says. "He calls them Mag-C rings like they're
just tools, but they feel diffcrent now."

I look at mine. The metal is warm against my finger,
humming so softly it almost matches Sam's breathing. "He
says they resonate when they're close. Guess that still means
something."

Lindsay smiles faintly. "Do you think they'd still work… if
we weren't in the same place?"

I shrug. "Maybe. Or maybe they just remind us we survived
another day."

She glances toward the truck bed where Sam lies motionless.
"He probably doesn't even realize they'll end up meaning
more than that."

"Yeah," I say quietly. "But he's right about one thing — they
pull together."

For a moment, we just listen — the hum of the forest, the
far-off river, Sam's slow breathing. The two rings pulse once
more in unison, then go still.

The silence that follows feels almost deliberate, as if the
night itself is holding its breath. Lindsay leans her head
against her knees, the glow from her ring fading until it is

only a reflection of the stars above. I watch Sam's chest rise and fall — shallow, uneven, but steady enough to count on.

"He'll wake up," I say quietly.

"I know," she murmurs. "I just hope it's still him when he does."

She hesitates, tracing her finger along the edge of her ring. "When I was a kid, my dog — Milo — gets hit by a car outside our house. He isn't breathing when I find him. I sit there in the street, talking to him like he can still hear me. I tell him I'll stay until he comes back." Her voice falters. "He does. Couple of minutes later, he gasps and starts whining. But after that, he's never quite the same. He'd stare at corners like he saw something we didn't."

I don't know what to say. The story lingers in the dark like smoke.

"I guess I'm doing the same thing now," she says. "Waiting for something to breathe again."

I nod. "Then we wait."

Before she can answer, Sam's voice comes from behind us — quiet, rasped.

"Touching story."

We turn. He is awake, eyes half-open, a smirk ghosting across his face.

"Sam!" Lindsay gasps, leaning toward him.

He winces, sitting up slowly. "What happened?"

"Your arm," I reply. "Infection. We gave you penicillin."

He flexes his fingers, eyes unfocused. "That explains the headache."

Lindsay laughs, half relief, half tears. "You scared us."

"Wouldn't be the first time," he says, managing a weak grin.

I open my mouth to say more, but the sound hits first — distant sirens cutting through the trees. Red and blue light shimmers faintly between the branches.

"They found us," Lindsay whispers.

Sam's expression hardens. "My phone," he says. "Give me my phone."

I hand it over carefully. The cracked screen flickers once, twice — then steadies to a faint blue pulse.

"Hold on," he says.

The air bends.
The light swallows everything.

And just like that — we are gone.

Chapter Eight

Year: 2080 — Markus

We stay inside the skeleton of what had once been an apartment tower. The wind comes through the shattered panels and sings in the elevator shaft, a slow metallic moan that changes pitch with the hour. We sleep in a corner room with no door, wrapped in thermal blankets I scavenged from a relief station two blocks over. At night, the magnetic storms roll in like silent auroras, green veins cutting across the dark. I wake to see Sam sitting near the window, the light flickering across his face, eyes fixed on something distant and unreadable.

The first days he barely speaks, his body shaking from the rift. But slowly, the color returns to him. The chip stops flaring behind his eyes. He can stand longer, walk without falling against the wall. One morning he even laughs when Lindsay hands him a cup of boiled rainwater and calls it coffee.

Outside, the city is still dying. There are blackouts that last days. The power grid flickers like a candle near its end. The old screens in the public squares show static — sometimes a message from the World Government, sometimes nothing at all. *"Exodus Initiative—Mars Habitation Phase Accelerated."* The same announcement loops through corrupted sound.

Sam taps into his archive once his strength returns. I remember how the room brightens with the pale light of his interface, the images bleeding through the air — maps of Mars, red dust plains, the metallic shimmer of orbiting stations.

"The core's unstable," he says, scrolling through fragments of scientific briefs. "They've been monitoring the magnetic drift for decades, but it's gotten worse. They're predicting total collapse within fifty years. Maybe twenty."

Lindsay sits beside him, her hands around the cracked ceramic mug. "So the world's ending," she says, like she's already accepted it.

Sam nods. "That's what they're planning for. Space stations. Mars colonies. Exodus fleets. No one left behind, they claim. But there's never enough room for everyone."

I don't say anything. I think about my own time, how people still argue about what the end might look like — fire or famine, divine or man-made. Now I am standing in the answer.

When Sam finally says we need to find Jex Titor, it doesn't sound like a mission — more like an instinct. "He'll know how to trace the interference," Sam says. "And we'll need a place to stay that isn't falling apart."

The next morning, we leave the tower. The air outside carries a faint metallic taste, like rust and ozone. We pass streets where glass has melted from heat storms, and signs half-buried in dust: *Orion Medical District, Sector 9 Transit, Civic Archive Closed.* Drones hover, directionless, their lights dimming and reigniting. On the horizon, the Mag-Train jerks along its rail like a wounded animal, stopping mid-air before crawling forward again.

Sam watches it, frowning. "The field's breaking down. Magnetism's eating itself."

We walk. It's safer that way. The Mag-Glides sputter and crash mid-turn, their riders thrown like sparks. People have abandoned vehicles altogether.

As we move through the city's outer sectors, we begin seeing them — the preachers. Some stand on overturned cargo crates, shouting into handheld speakers; others simply walk barefoot through the ash, whispering prayers. "The world cracks, the sky bends, repent!" one calls out as we pass. His eyes are wide and milk-white, his hands trembling in rhythm with the static hum of the air.

Lindsay slows down to look. "They really believe it," she murmurs.

Sam's voice is quiet. "Belief's all they have left."

I say nothing. Their chants remind me of my mother. She used to leave the television on late at night, the evangelists crying about judgment and rebirth. I am top of my class then — math, science, all the measurable things. I like numbers because they don't lie. Prophecy belongs to people who fear uncertainty. I remember thinking that if the end ever came, I'd explain it away with physics. But standing here, watching the sky ripple like a broken mirror, I'm not so sure anymore.

We move through the outskirts where the streets become gravel and weeds. The silence thickens. Sam carries his pack with one hand pressed to his temple, checking readings every few minutes. I see the tension in him — not pain now, but calculation, the kind that precedes risk.

When we reach the ridge where the old pine forest begins, the wind shifts. The smell of the sea — faint, chemical, distant — mixes with the scent of scorched bark. "The cabin's this way," Sam says.

We descend through the trees. The path is overgrown but still there, a memory of the world before. Every so often, static flickers through my vision from the interference in the air. I wonder if it's just an illusion or my own nerves misfiring.

By the time we see the cabin, dusk has fallen. It stands crooked against the slope, its windows clouded with dust. Sam raises his hand, signaling us to stop.

"Approach with caution," he says.

Lindsay and I don't need the order. It's instinct. Months of training, even from another life, live inside us. We circle the perimeter silently, scanning for movement. The grass crunches underfoot. I note every sound, every shift of air. Sam waits near the door, his hand resting over the small pistol on his belt.

When we regroup, he nods. "Clear."

Inside, the air is stale but dry. The last sunset spills through the cracks in the walls, turning the dust into gold threads. For the first time in weeks, the silence feels kind. We drop our packs. Lindsay finds an old kettle, rinses it with bottled water, and makes something close to coffee. The smell is bitter but familiar.

We sit around the table — if it can be called that, just a plank over two crates — and listen to the wind slide across the cabin. Sam stares at the small flicker of flame under the kettle. I think he is weighing the risk before he speaks.

"I'm going to contact Jex," he says finally. "Through the IMC."

"Is that safe?" I ask.

"Probably not. But if I encrypt it deep enough, they won't trace it."

He opens his interface. Thin blue light spreads across his face. His fingers move in short, deliberate gestures, like someone threading code through a lock. Then he speaks the message aloud as he types, a string of numbers and letters that mean nothing to us but everything to the man it's meant for:

"JJ-7A492. North ridge / 43N-106W in retrospect / dawn signal—C-78 clear. Old firepot intact. Awaiting lime-echo."

The screen dims. The message vanishes.

Lindsay pours the coffee into three chipped mugs. The steam rises and twists between us. For a while, no one speaks. Then she says, "Do you think there's something after all this?"

Sam looks at her. "You mean after the world?"

"After us."

He thinks for a long moment. "I used to think time was the only constant — that it couldn't end, only bend. But if that's true, maybe we don't end either. Maybe we just... move, maybe time holds us until we're ready to let go."

I turn the cup in my hands. "In my time, people argued about heaven. I never cared much. I just wanted to understand how things worked. Equations, cause and effect. But standing here, I think maybe understanding isn't the point."

Lindsay smiles faintly. "Then what is?"

"Maybe it's just not being alone when it happens like having friends and family."

Sam looks down into his cup. "Then we're doing alright."

The wind presses against the windows, a low moan that might be words. We sit there a long time, the three of us, holding on to something small and warm.

Lindsay smiles faintly, the kind of smile that lives more in the eyes than the mouth. Outside, the wind moves through the pines, making the cabin breathe with each gust — old boards flexing, settling, whispering. For a moment, it feels almost safe.

Then Lindsay's voice breaks the quiet. "Sam," she says softly. "That woman — Juliette. Is she still alive? In this time?"

Sam doesn't answer right away. He looks toward the window, where the last light is fading. "I checked," he says finally. "While I was bedridden. Looked her up in the archives."

Lindsay sets her cup down gently. "And?"

"She lived longer than before," he says. "Months longer; almost a year. She makes it through the first collapse, but not the second. Dies during the southern blackout, in the riots. There isn't much left after that."

The silence that follows isn't heavy — just tired. The kind that comes when truth has nothing left to take.

Lindsay nods slowly. "At least she made it further."

Sam gives a slight nod, eyes still on the window. "*Further*," he says, almost to himself.

I think about what that word means — how time keeps handing out extensions, not miracles. You can stretch a life, bend it, replay it, but the ending still waits somewhere, quiet and patient. Maybe living longer isn't the same as being saved. Maybe nothing really is; loss folds into time — how it doesn't end, just changes shape.

The wind eases. The fire dims. For a heartbeat, everything stills — the kind of stillness that feels deliberate, like the world pausing to listen.

Lindsay traces a finger around the rim of her mug. "You know," she says softly, "if we ever make it out of this, I'm opening the first café on Mars. I'll call it *The Paradox*."

Sam looks up. "The Paradox?"

"Yeah." She smiles. "A place for people who keep cheating the clock. You'd have your own drink — double-shot espresso with a side of existential crisis."

He almost smiles, that ghost of expression that passes for laughter in him. "Make it strong," he says.

"Always," she replies.

For a moment, the world outside seems lighter. I can almost forget the hum of the magnetic storms or the taste of metal in the air. The sound of the kettle cooling is the only clock that matters.

I stare at the steam rising between us and think about the word further again — how it is both a direction and a distance. We keep going further: through centuries, through ruins, through whatever counts as hope. And yet it feels like we're standing in the same place, orbiting our own endings.

The light in the room thins to gray. Dust hangs in the air, drifting through the faint glow of the dying fire. Somewhere outside, a branch taps against the roof in a slow rhythm, like the world itself trying to speak.

Lindsay leans forward, resting her chin in her hands. "Do you ever think we'll ever stop altering?"

Sam doesn't answer. His gaze follows the smoke spiraling toward the ceiling. "Stopping means giving up," he says finally.

"Maybe not," she says. "Maybe it just means resting long enough to see if things naturally get better."

I watch the two of them — her eyes bright in the half-light, his shadow fixed against the wall like something separate from him. For a moment, they look almost ordinary. Three people drinking coffee in a cabin while the world outside quietly dissolves.

The wind rises again, pushing at the walls until the boards shiver. I think of my parents and their late-night talks about faith — how they said the world could end a thousand ways, but the heart would always keep pretending it was safe. Maybe that's our last defense: pretending.

Lindsay gives a small laugh. "You know, I'd name one of the drinks after you too, Markus."

"Yeah?"

"Mm-hmm. Black coffee, no sugar. I'd call it *The Realist*."

I smile. "Then no one would order it."

She shrugs. "Somebody has to keep the menu honest."

Even Sam smiles at that — the faintest curve at the corner of his mouth.

Outside, the wind settles again. The quiet stretches, soft and uneasy. I can feel the temperature drop, the cold sneaking in through the seams of the wood. The world beyond the walls waits, breathing with us.

Then comes the knock.

I hear the knock before the others do, three slow taps that sound like somebody measuring the room. Sam stands, eyes already on the door. Lindsay's hand tightens around her cup until the rim clicks. I feel the air change — the way it gets just before a storm, when the trees hold their breath.

Sam doesn't ask who it is. He moves with that quiet steadiness that means his mind has already run the math and found all the exits with his pistol in hand. He slides the latch. The door opens to night and a man shaped like a long road.

"Jex," Sam says.

The man smiles without showing teeth. "Took you long enough to call," he says, and his voice carries the dust of a hundred miles.

For a second none of us move. Then Jex steps in, shuts the door with his heel, and opens his arms the way people do when they're tired of standing alone. Sam hugs him hard, a rare break in the surface. Lindsay and I freeze — not sure what we are to him, what he is to us.

"Come here," Jex says. "I feel like we're family."

We step in. His jacket smells like rain caught in old canvas. He hugs without asking anything from the hug. When he lets go, he looks at us one by one, studying, mapping. There's gray at his temples now, the kind earned by heat and bad news.

"I got your coded ping," he says to Sam. "North ridge, dawn signal; but actually South. So, that time we were on the run; didn't get far."

"What happened?" Sam asks.

"Got detained," Jex says, easy as if describing the weather. "Checkpoint sweep. Wrong face in the wrong place. They gave me a choice: jail or a uniform. I took the uniform."

He pulls a folded cloth from his pocket and sets it on the table like a poker chip. It's a patch, black field with a white ring around a small blue planet. Inside the ring: three lines forming a trident. The letters beneath read: Civic Stabilization Branch.

"One World Government calls it the *Unified Civic Authority*," he says. "UCA. I was in their standard branch—street-level deployments, disaster corridors, convoy escorts. One-year mandatory cycle." He glances at Sam. "Which matches how long you were gone, I take it."

"You couldn't get to the cabin," Sam says. "And yeah, roughly a year."

Jex shakes his head. "No leave the first six months. After that I tried. But we were glued to magnetism incidents and power collapses. The sky went bad, the rails went worse. You saw what the Mag-Lines look like—drunk snakes. Even the drones can't hold a line anymore."

He sits, and the chair creaks in a slow, tired way. "I learned where I could. The real things — the ones you care about — live under a different roof. S.T.T."

"What's S.T.T.?" Lindsay asks.

"*Science of Time Transport*," Jex says. "Publicly: a research consortium built from the remnants of defense labs. Privately: the government's best guess at catching up to you. They don't call it time travel, though. Can't. Not until they can prove where and when something lands."

"You got inside?" I ask.

"I got near," he says. "We shared perimeter security during grid failures. Sometimes I slipped the line and watched from catwalks. Saw enough to know what they do — and what they can't."

Sam leans forward. "Tell me."

"They started with animals," Jex says. "Rats, strays, butcher's goats. Transport lattices built into a concrete floor — 13 by 13 coils with a central well. They tune a field, pulse it, and the animals... twitch out of the world." He pinches his fingers together and pops the air. "Not burned. Not crushed. Just gone. Sometimes they reappear across the room with singed fur and eyes unfocused. Sometimes not at all."

"Teleportation," I remark.

"Transport," Jex corrects. "They won't say 'teleportation' because they can't keep it stable, and they won't say 'time' because they can't prove displacement across it. But the part that makes them sweat isn't the going. It's the staying gone."

We wait.

"They call it teleportation contagion," he says. "One subject goes. Another in the same pen goes five seconds later without being pulsed. Then another. The field leaves a residue — call it a wake — somehow priming the nervous system to catch the next wave. They cage one goat, pulse another in a different room, and the first goat twitches at nothing and blinks out like a bad channel. Contagion jumps physical barriers. They lock doors, wrap cages in mu-metal, ground the floors. It slows, but doesn't stop."

Lindsay's mouth opens, then closes. I feel a cold line trace my spine.

Jex looks at Sam. "Sound familiar?"

Sam's expression doesn't move, but something behind his eyes does. "Markus. Lindsay," he says quietly. "The tether."

Jex nods. "Exactly. Whatever your chip does, whatever storm stitched you to each other, S.T.T. sees the same pattern in animals. You zap. They zap. It's not consent. It's exposure."

"Did they find a way to stop it?" I ask.

"They find two ways to smother it," Jex says. "First, a serum — a serum built from counter-field proteins pulled off a radiation fungus. They inject it before trials. It doesn't cure the tendency, but it reduces the cascade. Subjects are less likely to catch the wave from each other."

"And the second?" Sam asks.

"A flux-weave," he says. "Fabric filaments grown with a paramagnetic lattice. Wear it and the body's field holds shape better when the room's spinning. They line cages with it. Contagion dips. Not gone. Lower. Think of it as rebar for the aura."

Lindsay's eyebrows rise. "Aura?"

"Call it biofield if you want the lab word," Jex says. "Point is: it's a net that keeps you from slipping."

"And you think this could help us," Sam says.

"I think the serum and the weave together could cut the tether," Jex says. "Or at least dull it. If Markus and Lindsay dose up and suit up, they might stop following you when you jump."

Silence takes a slow breath. Fire pops, the kettle clicks, the cabin's bones settle like an animal sighing.

I swallow. "What if we don't want to cut it."

They both look at me. I don't mean to sound like I'm standing on a cliff, but it comes out that way.

"I want to stay with Lindsay," I admit. The words surprise me with how plain they are. "If Sam time travels, I don't want to watch him vanish and wait for news."

Lindsay reaches for my hand. There's a steadiness in her grip that tells me she's already thought all this through and arrived somewhere difficult.

"Your Aunt Carol," she says softly. "You told me about her. You're all she's got."

I look at the floorboards, old knots like closed eyes. "I know," I say. The two words have the weight of a door I can't open and can't ignore.

Sam stands and sets a hand on Jex's shoulder. "Walk with me," he says. The two of them step out onto the porch, and wind moves the pines like a quiet crowd shifting its weight.

Lindsay and I sit without speaking. She rubs her thumb along the rim of her cup the way people polish thoughts. I watch the shadow of the door and try to read a conversation from the shapes of shoulders and hands. Once, Sam's face blurs with something I don't like. Dismay, maybe. The kind you get when a known equation develops a new term you don't have the symbols for.

Jex comes back in first. "We need to eat," he says. "Thinking on empty makes it hard for everyone."

"I'll go," I look over at Lindsay.

"So will I," Jex says. "We'll check the service road stores, see what the storm left behind. If we get lucky, I'll scare some potential game out of a rust patch."

Sam explains earlier to me that hunting is illegal, technically. But the drones that would have cared are blind now, their lenses fogged by a world that has forgotten the trick of being a world.

Lindsay layers more wood on the coals. "Be careful," she says.

"Always," Jex says. He cuts a thin smile at Sam. "If you break, don't do it while we're gone."

Sam tries to smile back. He doesn't make it all the way.

We take the ridge down toward the old service road. Needles break under our boots with a soft crackle. The air has that metallic taste again, like the world carries a battery on its tongue. Jex walks with hands easy at his sides, the way people do when they've had to carry too much weight for too long and learn to hide it.

"I never said thank you," I tell him. "Back at the apartment. You opened the door first."

He shrugs. "Somebody has to."

We find the service road half-buried in blown dirt. An old cart lies on its side in the ditch. Jex rights it with a grunt and checks the wheels. Two still turn.

"What's your full name?" I ask, pushing as we move trying to make conversation.

He laughs quietly. "Thought Sam told you."

"He calls you Jex."

"Everybody does," he says. "It's a tie from two names. John Jex Titor. My father has a joke about it — something about time turning back on itself so you could be your own good ancestor. He likes paradoxes. The kind that make you dizzy if you stare too long."

He says it like it's a story he's told often enough to sand off all the sharp parts, but I can see one edge catching light behind his eyes.

"Your parents?" I ask.

"Gone," he says, not unkindly. "Most people's are. Or maybe they're somewhere on an *Exodus* station stacking air filters. Doesn't matter. In this time, you let go of the dead or you drink them like bad water."

We reach a small cluster of storefronts with windows boarded in a neat kind of grief. Jex pries a loose panel and slides inside. I follow. Dust lies on everything like a final coat of paint. We find a storage room and two crates of canned beans, one of peaches in heavy syrup, and a row of noodles stiff as straw.

We load the cart.

"You and Lindsay," Jex says after a while. "Real or surviving together until you figure out if it's real?"

"Both," I say. "In my time I could measure things until they behaved. Here I just hold on and pray with people who don't like the word 'pray'."

"Heard worse plans," he says. He reaches into a pocket and pulls out something small and metallic. The light in the back room is bad, but I can see the simple clean line of his vintage lighter now lighting the way.

"The Mag-C rings," I say. "I gave one to her," I add, sudden heat in my face like I have to justify a gesture to a man I barely know.

"I remember the day I bought them. Good morning. Bad afternoon. Walked the whole Central Market with someone who thought rules were only suggestions. She laughed. She tried on hats she didn't intend to pay for. Then she saw somebody who laughed louder." He lifts a shoulder. "Life does what it does."

"Do you miss her?" I ask.

"Sometimes I miss the idea of the day," he says. "Not the person. Memory edits. Don't trust first cuts."

He glances at the ring on my finger. "You did right. People need anchors when the sky forgets its job."

Outside, Jex surprises a rabbit from a tangle of dead nettle and takes it with a clean throw of his utility blade. He moves like he's practiced on shadows and made peace with the fact that shadows bleed.

"You were honest back there," he says as we start back, the cart rattling lightly. "Saying you want to stay with her. Most men circle the truth until it gets tired and sits down."

"I don't want to leave her," I say, and there is no uncertainty in it. "But I don't want to be the kind of man who abandons his aunt either."

Jex studies me like he already knows the outcome.

"Here's what I know," he says. "Love is a door and a lock at once. You learn when to open and when to hold. If you stay, you stay with your whole body. If you go, don't build a chapel out of the guilt."

"Did you ever build one?"

"Couple," he says. "Burned them all. Smoke smells the same, no matter what you pray to."

We walk in silence for a while. The trees sing again — that slow elevator-shaft moan, wind threading itself through the throat of the forest.

"What about Juliette?" I ask finally. "Sam's girl."

Jex's face doesn't change, but the lines around his mouth set themselves closer together. "I don't know her," he says. "Only the contour of her in Sam's sentences. The way he carries her like a pocket weight he checks ten times a day. His voice goes quiet when he says her name. That's all I need to know."

We reach the cabin just as the light is folding itself into the ground. Lindsay bursts from the doorway and sprints toward us, hair loose, eyes wide in a way I've never seen.

"Hurry," she says, breath snapping the word in two. "It's Sam."

We run. Inside, Sam lies on the floor, body rigid, hands clawed as if he's trying to hold the floor down to keep himself from floating away. His eyes are open and not seeing, the blue gone pale with too much sky inside.

"Hold his shoulders," Jex says, already at Sam's side. He slides a hand beneath Sam's head so it won't beat the boards and with the other digs for the phone at Sam's belt. He presses it to Sam's palm.

"Reset," Jex says. "Now."

I've seen Sam hit reset before, the way a man hits a panic button inside his own bones. But he isn't there to do it. Jex takes Sam's thumb, presses it to the sensor, and speaks into the device — low, even, like he's talking to a skittish animal.

"IMC override, manual assist," he says. "Reset."

The phone vibrates. A low thrum passes through the cabin, through us. Sam's back arches, then his body drops all at once, like a string cut. His breathing comes in ragged pulls. His eyes blink and find the room again, as if he's been underwater and just remembered what air is named.

Lindsay is on her knees, her hands on his face. "Sam," she says. "Look at me."

He does. The light in him comes back in small pieces, like coals remembering fire.

"What was that?" I ask. My voice sounds far away.

"His IMC," Jex says. "Chip went wild. The field in his head spiked, and his body tried to follow someplace it couldn't. He needs a buffer. He needs sleep that isn't a battlefield."

Sam swallows. His throat works around the word he chooses. "I was gone," he says.

"No," Lindsay whispers, but it comes out like a wish.

"I was gone," he says again, and this time the word is a place. "Not my body. Something else. My mind wrapped in heat. Thought I was dreaming. Then I knew I wasn't."

Jex helps him sit, slow and careful. Sam stares past us a moment, anywhere people look when the thing they saw doesn't leave them entirely.

"Tell it," Jex says softly.

Sam's eyes find the table, as if truth needs wood under it to stand.

"I was on a ridge made of ash that wasn't ash," he says. "There was no wind. There couldn't be. The sky was a black sheet with a hole cut in it. The Earth was…" He stops. His mouth presses shut, not to hold back tears, but to hold back a shape.

"Say it," Jex says. There's no cruelty in it.

"Broken," Sam says. "In half. Not tidy. Torn. One side red glass, one side a bruise. The core smokes like a dying star. No water, just seams where oceans used to argue with land. I move without feet. I realize — I'm not in time. I'm near it. Like standing behind a curtain and seeing shadows move."

"How far?" I ask. My voice becomes the math voice again without my permission.

"Far enough for the stations to be dust," he says. "Far enough that names don't matter. I thought it was nothing. Then I saw the curve of a Mag-Train rail suspended over nothing, broken in a way gravity should have refused. A sign: *Orion District*. It floated, burned, then turned to a line of embers and was gone."

Silence walks through the room and sits in every chair.

"We have to save this world," Sam says.

There's no drama in it. No speech. Just a line thick with a man's private vow.

Jex nods once, like he's saluting something only he can see. "Then we need a plan that doesn't get you killed in the first hour," he says. "Your chip is a bomb you keep disarming by hand."

"We don't leave," I say. It surprises me, how clear the words are. "Not yet. We save this place first. Then we hunt your serum and weave and figure how to cut the tether enough to get us home."

"I agree," Lindsay says. There's a ring of steel in her voice. She hasn't grown armor. She's grown spine.

Jex looks from her to me to Sam. "All right," he says. "We start with what we can steal. We get you the flux-weave and the serum and whatever field dampeners S.T.T. keeps for rainy days. I have a path into their outer labs. We don't break their door. We borrow their keys."

"And the contagion?" I ask. "If it's really a wake that catches bodies, not just machines."

"Then we stay out of each other's way to avoid a slipstream; if you ever have to jump out of this time year make sure I'm not too close, just do me that favor," Jex says. "We move smart. We don't get near any of those experimental animals if we don't have to."

He turns to Sam. "You won't survive a dozen more spikes like that. The IMC will chew through whatever's left of your margin. I won't talk to you like you're made of glass, but I'll say it plain: you're running on credit."

Sam's jaw sets. "We'll push through," he says. "I take them home then we save this world."

Home hangs in the air like a word that has to be spelled with hands while trying to save a world without knowing if it's possible. If there is one thing in this world I trust not to falter, it's Sam's relentlessness for absolution.

Jex sets the cans on the table, lines them into simple order, then takes a breath that makes him look younger for a second. "Eat first," he says. "Plan after. The worst mistakes I've made were on an empty stomach."

We eat. Peaches in syrup taste like a childhood I remember that I've never had. Lindsay carves the rabbit with small movements that tell me she's deciding not to think about what it had been before it was a meal. The cabin warms and the wind loses its edge.

After, Jex spreads a torn map on the table — old paper, new ink. Circles and crossed lines, a set of marks that look like music written by somebody who likes geometry more than notes.

"S.T.T. has three satellite sites," he says. "Primary's off-limits unless you want to meet people who practice their aim on holidays. But the *Ravel Annex* handles field gear. Smaller staff. They move their flux-weave there for integration runs. We get in. We take enough for two suits, maybe three if its possible. We find a cold-storage locker for serum — vials marked with a red tag and a date. Keep them upright. They don't like heat."

"How do we get in?" I ask.

"By looking like the kind of problem the world's too tired to solve," Jex says. "Badged van, wrong paperwork, right posture. Night shift. Magnetism softens cameras. Add a distraction two blocks away — false grid flare. That buys us seven minutes before they realize the flare is static."

"You've done worse with less," Sam says, not quite a question.

"I've done stupid with nothing," Jex says. "I'd like to try smart for once."

Lindsay traces one of the circles. "And after?"

"After we get your bodies quiet," Jex says. "Then we listen for the place where your world can be saved from this one. Don't make the mistake of thinking there's only one knot to cut. The planet's failing because the core is drunk and the grid is tired and the people are afraid. You don't fix that with a single heroic lever. You fix it with a thousand small corrects. You fix it by making sure there's a future for any lever to be pulled."

Outside, the wind lays itself down. The cabin listens to us and seems to approve. Sam leans back and shuts his eyes like a man who still doesn't trust sleep but has decided to let it borrow him for a while.

I step outside and look up through the dark ribs of the trees. The sky is a table where someone has spilled salt and tried to sweep it back into the shaker. You can see the trail where the stars have been. More like scattered ink now.

Lindsay comes to stand beside me. She doesn't say anything. She doesn't need to.

"Your Aunt Carol," she says at last, almost a question.

"I'll find a way to be both men," I state. "The one who stays. The one who goes."

"They don't usually live in the same house," she says with a smile.

"They will," I respond, and it feels like a promise I owe the man I want to be.

We go back in. Jex is still bent over the map, marking paths like a cartographer of storms. Sam sleeps with one hand near his phone, the way a soldier sleeps with fingers brushing steel.

I sit and watch them both. The man who has made war with time and the man who has learned to sit still long enough to find him again. Outside, the pines whisper, and for once their song doesn't sound like a warning. It sounds like a plan beginning.

Chapter Nine
Year: 2080 — Markus

Morning comes gray and thin, light spilling through the cracks in the blinds like ash. The air smells of wood smoke and metal. I wake to the sound of wind working its way through the eaves. Lindsay lies beside me, curled against my chest, her hand caught in the fabric of my shirt as if the night tries to pull her away and she doesn't let go.

For a moment, the world seems almost clean again. Quiet. I can pretend the noise of the city, the hum of failing grids, the low ache of magnetism gone sour—none of it exists here. Only her breathing, steady and small.

Then I hear Sam's voice. Low. Focused.

He is at the table with Jex, a spread of maps and half-burned notes before them. Jex's cigarette glows like a tiny dying sun. They speak in short sentences, the way men do when the clock is close to running out.

"We can't save it this way," Jex says. "You know that."

"There's always another way," Sam replies. "We just haven't found it yet."

Their voices carry through the quiet cabin, and something in me tightens. I've heard enough of these late-night talks—the kind that make you realize you're not part of the plan, only orbiting around it.

Sam turns as if sensing I'm awake. He gives a brief nod. "Morning, Markus."

"Morning," I say, sitting up. The wood floor is cold under my feet.

Lindsay stirs beside me and blinks toward the light. "What time is it?"

"Too early for hope," Jex mutters.

Sam ignores him. "We move today," he says. "The window's small, and the city's surveillance grid will be weaker than usual. We take the serum and the flux weave, get out, and then figure out how to fix what's left of the world."

Lindsay pulls her hair into a knot and says nothing. Her eyes look clearer than mine. She stopped pretending this was an adventure a long time ago.

Jex tosses a cigarette across the table. "You smoke, Sam?"

"Not anymore," Sam says, catching it anyway.

"Now's the time to start again," Jex says, lighting his own and tossing the lighter over. It clatters across the wood. Sam picks it up, runs his thumb over the engraving.

Light 'em if you got 'em.

He smiles faintly. "Old soldier saying."

"Old world saying," Jex corrects. "Picked it up from a junk dealer who didn't know what it meant."

"Everything's junk now," Sam says, and lights the cigarette. The smoke curls upward, joining the gray air.

He looks back at me and Lindsay. "You two ready?"

"As we'll ever be," I say.

Jex leans over the table and unrolls a thick sheet of plastic laminate—schematics of the S.T.T. compound. Lines, grids, access points. "We'll need explosives," he says. "Homemade stuff. Nothing fancy."

Sam nods. "You have what we need?"

"Under the cabin," Jex says. "Weapons too. Rifles, handguns. Took them from my garrison during the riots. Nobody left to miss them back then."

Sam's eyes flick toward the window, where light breaks over the trees. "We do this fast," he says. "In and out before the next shift starts."

I watch his hands move across the map, tracing paths like veins. "Sector Two first," he says. "That's where we bring down the grid. It'll blind their surveillance long enough for us to hit the compound."

"And the distraction?" I ask, already assuming Sam wants to run this mission like our previous one.

"Old factory half a mile from the front gate," Jex says. "We light it up. Fire'll draw them off."

I'm right.

"Won't the drones handle it?" Lindsay asks.

Jex shakes his head. "They would, if the city wasn't falling apart. Magnetism's shot. Machines keep shorting out. Firefighters are just old metal ghosts now."

Lindsay glances at me. "So the humans go instead."

"That's the idea," Sam says. "They'll keep it old-fashion."

I stand and walk toward the small window. Outside, the sky looks bruised. The hum of the city in the distance is faint, like a heart that hasn't decided if it wants to keep beating.

Jex's voice comes again, low and quick. "We hit the grid at 0900. Then the compound. Expect resistance."

"Always do," Sam says.

We load the weapons in silence. The sound of metal against wood is steady, rhythmic. Lindsay handles each rifle like she's done it before—because she has. She doesn't look at me once.

When we're ready, we step outside. The cold bites at our faces. The wind carries a strange hum through the branches, the same hum that always comes before something breaks.

Sam leads. Jex carries the bag of homemade charges. Lindsay and I follow close, boots crunching over the frost.

The road to the city is quiet. No cars. No sound but the wind and the low whine of distant machinery.

By the time we reach the edge of Sector Two, the light has changed. It's harsher now, fractured by dust and the faint shimmer of magnetic fields gone wrong. The power station looms ahead—huge, skeletal, wires drooping like veins.

Jex crouches behind a wall and starts setting the charges. "Once we light this, we have ten minutes to clear the area."

Sam checks his watch. "Plenty."

The air smells of ozone and metal. The hum grows louder, pulsing through my chest.

"Ready?" Sam asks.

Jex nods, stands, and presses the trigger. The explosion rolls through the air, slow at first, then cracking like thunder. Smoke rises, black and heavy.

Lights across the city flicker, then die. The hum vanishes.

"Go," Sam says.

We run. Down the main street, through alleys half-eaten by rust. The S.T.T. compound rises in the distance, all sharp lines and concrete teeth.

Jex's clearance badge gets us through the first gate. The scanner buzzes, flickers, then turns green. "Told you," he mutters.

Inside, the corridors are sterile and bright, too clean for a world falling apart. We move fast, heads down. For a moment, it seems like maybe we'll walk right through.

Then we hear the shout.

"Hold up! Identification!"

Two military police at the far end. Their rifles are already up.

Jex raises his hands. "We're on a maintenance detail! Power grid failure!"

They don't buy it. One steps forward, eyes narrowing. "Who authorized—"

The lights flicker. The hum returns, stuttering. Then one of the guards' radios hisses, a burst of static.

Lindsay moves first. Her hand brushes my arm—warning.
Then she steps forward, voice smooth, calm. "You don't
have time to verify. Sector Two's burning. You want the
whole place offline?"

They hesitate.

Then one of them sees the rifle slung under my coat.

"Drop it!" he shouts.

Too late. The shot cracks through the corridor. Jex reacts.
The first guard goes down.

Chaos follows.

Alarms blare for a second, then die again, power choking
midstream. Smoke drifts from the wiring overhead.

"Cover!" Sam shouts.

We drop behind a stack of metal crates. Bullets tear into the
walls, splinters of plaster flying. I can taste the dust, the iron.

Lindsay returns fire, short bursts. Jex curses under his
breath, checking his weapon. "They're calling for backup!"

"Not if the comms are down," Sam says.

We move—inch by inch, across the corridor. The air is thick,
vibrating with noise and heat. More soldiers appear at the far
end.

"They're flanking!" Jex shouts.

"Keep moving!" Sam yells.

We cut through a side passage, into a dim stairwell that smells of oil and smoke. My heart is a drum in my chest. I can hear Lindsay breathing hard behind me.

The next hallway opens into a lab sector—white walls, glass doors shattered from the shockwaves. We slip through the wreckage.

"Left wing!" Jex calls. "That's where the lab-vault is!"

We reach a sealed door with a keypad. Jex kneels, working fast. Sparks light his face.

"Hurry," Sam says.

"I'm trying," Jex growls. "System's old. Doesn't like me."

A burst of gunfire from the hall behind us. Bullets chew through glass. Lindsay fires back.

"Now, Jex!" I shout.

The door beeps, clicks open.

We stumble inside, slam it shut, destroy the keypad control, and shove a desk against it.

The lab is empty except for the humming servers and one man crouched behind a desk.

"Hands where I can see them!" Sam barks.

The man stands slowly, trembling. His glasses catch the flicker of the emergency lights.

"Dr. Bresner," Jex says quietly.

Recognition flashes in the man's eyes. "You. You were thrown out of here months ago."

"And you're still here," Jex says.

Then the doctor's gaze shifts. He looks past Jex, at Sam. His mouth falls open. "It's you."

Sam freezes. "You've got me mistaken for someone else."

"No," Bresner says. "We've seen you. The footage. You disappear. You're in the reports—the anomalies."

Sam's jaw tightens. "Where's the serum and flux weave?"

Bresner doesn't answer.

Jex steps forward. "Answer him."

The doctor points shakily to a locked cabinet. "There. But if you take it, they'll come for you. They'll know."

"They already know," Sam says.

Jex breaks the lock and grabs two vials, both glowing faintly blue with a red tag. He stuffs them into his bag along with some flux weave, but not enough.

"We've got it!" he shouts.

The pounding on the door starts then—boots, shouts, metal striking metal.

Sam turns. "Markus, set a charge on that wall. We're not using the front door."

I pull a sticky bomb from my pack and slap it against the concrete, the type of bomb Jex trains us how to make. The timer blinks red.

"Everyone back!"

The explosion tears through the lab, the wall collapsing into open air. Smoke and dust pour in, sunlight slicing through it like gold through ash.

We run toward the opening—then Bresner's voice rises behind us.

"Wait! You can't just leave!"

Sam turns, gun still raised. "We've got what we came for."

"No!" Bresner shouts. "You don't understand. The planet—its core is dying. We need cold fusion!"

We freeze. The words hang there, heavy as stone.

Sam lowers his gun slowly. "Explain."

Bresner's eyes are wild behind the lenses, as if the emergency lights have set fire to whatever courage he has left. "We've modeled it for years," he says, the words tumbling. "The magnetosphere isn't just weakening; it's warping. It feeds back into the core like infection. Heat builds, release fails, iron flow goes strange. We can't vent it. The planet convulses by degrees, like a fever that won't break."

I feel the floor under my boots, the faint tremor that never quite leaves this city. Machines cough somewhere in the ducts overhead. The air in the lab smells of hot wiring and dust. Time runs its sickness through everything here—like rust that learned to count.

"What do you need?" Sam says, not a question, a blade.

"Cold fusion," Bresner says. "Portable. Not to help—" His voice cracks and then steadies. "To stop. You inject stabilized packets into the mantle vents. Dozens, then hundreds. They sink, convert flux to gentle heat, bleed pressure off the cycle. We almost have the models just in case for such a disaster; just how we plan for many other scenarios, then the ban comes in '55. They erase the data, burn the archives, take the people."

"Erased," Jex says, with that dry soldier's laugh that never reaches his eyes. "That's the word for anything they want to keep."

Bresner looks at Sam the way a man looks at a rope lowered into a well. "You can go to other years."

Sam doesn't deny it. He takes a breath, and the smoke from the blown wall moves in slow ribbons around him. "Where."

"1979," the doctor says. "Before the ban. There was a trial at the *Marigold Array*—private consortium off the coast—" He stops himself, shakes his head. "It won't matter. They scrub the records later. But the prototype exists. Even if the device is gone, the data isn't. It can't be. Someone saves it."

"We can get it," Sam says. There's no promise in the voice, but the shape of one lingers there.

Bresner nods quickly, as if convincing himself it's possible. "There's an old botanical dome in Sector Nine," he says. "Used to be part of a research compound. The structure's still sealed—no active power, no surveillance. The generators kick once every few days when the grid surges, that's all."

He runs a hand through his hair, eyes flicking toward the floor. "Inside, there's a central planter. Concrete bed, about two meters across. Leave the data drive inside a black toolbox under the soil there. When the surge hits, the heat will mask your signal. I'll come for it within the hour."

"It can't be done in an hour," Sam says. "Thirty days—or less. That's how it'll be done."

Bresner hesitates, swallowing hard. "Fine. Just don't wait longer than that. Every week the field gets worse. The system's… unpredictable."

Sam gives a short nod. The grow-lights overhead flicker once and go out, leaving the two men in the thin gray of morning.

"We'll make the time," Sam says, and I see the way his hand closes once, the way he places it flat on the table after, steadying the world or himself. "We have more of it than most. And less."

The door we barricaded groans under a strike. Metal
screams. Jex shoulders his bag, the clink of vials tucked in
canvas a small, bright sound. "We're done here," he says.

Sam looks at the doctor a moment longer. Something passes
through his face—pity or recognition or just the measure of
a man under bad skies. He holsters his gun. "Keep your head
down, Doctor. They'll blame you anyway."

"They already do," Bresner says with a hollow laugh.

We move for the hole. The lab's instruments click and
stutter as the power hits and misses like a dying heart. I set
another charge at the threshold in case we need to bury our
way out. We drop into the throat of the building where the
wall has fallen, boots sliding in powdered stone.

The outside air feels colder, thinner. It carries the faint
copper taste of blood from somewhere I can't name. We cut
across a maintenance yard broken by weeds and shattered
pallets. Sirens try to rise and fail, then rise again, sickly.
Above us the sky wears a bruise the color of old slate. The
long antennas on the rooftop shiver and give no signal.

"Left," Jex calls, and we take it, running under a trellis of
ductwork slick with condensation. I hear our breathing, four
separate engines beating toward a single goal. Behind us a
squad pours through the torn lab, figures black against white
dust, rifles up.

We clear a service corridor that smells of mineral cold and
burnt plastic and hit a door that will not read the badge, will
not read anything. Jex sets a charge the size of a fist and

blows the lock. The door sighs open like a lung that's been underwater too long.

Bullets find the walls around us and send chips singing. A shard cuts my cheek. It feels warm and then cold. I do not touch it. We move through.

Down another hall, bodies of old machines line the walls, their screens long dead, their trays stuck open like the mouths of fish that drowned on land. A fan turns, then stops, then turns again, as if deciding whether to live in this world or not. Every failure in the building seems to occur with a memory of itself. Time has taught the machines how to die by degrees.

At a fork, Sam doesn't hesitate. We take the darker side, the one with water on the floor. The other leads toward voices rising and the harsh bark of commands. I see the calculation in Sam's shoulders, the cut through the noise in his eyes. He can read a building the way other men read maps. The lighter weight sits in his pocket, I know, little metal joke against the gravity he carries.

We reach a stairwell that tunnels down and take it two flights. The handrail shocks me when I touch it—static like a wasp's sting. The power grid is throwing sparks at random, like a sick brain firing.

Below, a door with EXIT painted in a color that no longer looks like escape. Jex pushes through into a loading bay gouged by tire tracks and long neglect. A roll-up gate stutters halfway when we try to raise it and then dies.

"Help me," Sam says, and the three of us lift it by hand. Metal screams again. The gate rises far enough for us to belly under.

Outside, the rear of the compound breathes machine heat. Pipes run along the wall and exhale in thin steam. The yard beyond lies empty except for a dead forklift leaned at an angle, as if time has struck it and left it listing.

"On me," Sam says.

We run along the wall. Boots on grit. Shadows flicker behind the smoked glass of an office. A figure moves and then doesn't. Maybe their grid freezes him mid-frame; maybe I remember him before he acts. That's how the world feels these days—like a movie you've seen out of order and still love because the scenes fit like bones.

A shout. Then three military police break into the yard from the right and we dive behind the forklift. The first shot snaps open the forklift's window. Glass ticks at our backs.

Lindsay leans out, braces, and fires once, then twice. One of the MPs twists and goes down. The second ducks into cover. The third fires blind, bullets eating the paint off the forklift's mast.

I count the seconds it takes for him to breathe and then lean out and fire low. His leg folds. He makes a sound that has more surprise than pain in it. The second pops up and I hear the dry note of Jex's rifle answer him. He falls back into the shadow he tries to become.

"Go," Jex says, voice flat with professional urgency. "We won't get gifts like that again."

We cross the yard in a broken sprint. A siren somewhere finds its throat and keeps it. The fence at the back has a service gate with an old manual latch. When I throw it, it catches and throws me back a memory: the night in my own century when a door does the same and I laugh. There is rain then, and the sound of a train that isn't stopping. Time is an infection, I think again, because it never passes through clean. It leaves a film of itself on the next hour, and the next.

We reach the road, a service lane that bends behind a row of half-built units. The pavement has settled into a scalloped kind of failure. Our getaway car waits in the lee of a wall: a boxy four-door that has seen better decades and still has all of them in its bones. The paint is a humble gray the color of a middle distance. If you don't want to be seen, you pick a car that looks like furniture.

Sam takes the driver's seat. Jex goes shotgun. Lindsay and I slide into the back. As soon as the doors latch, the world outside feels as if it has stepped one pace farther away.

The engine turns. Coughs. Catches. The dash lights flicker in a private language and then agree on what they mean to be. Sam drives us out in second gear, slow enough to look like we belong to the day, fast enough to get us to one that will still have us.

Behind us the compound sets up a racket that tries to sound like control. Control in the face of defeat. In front, the road lifts and falls in those shallow waves, the city a wrecked harbor. Every antenna we pass trembles like it wants to shake free and walk home.

No one speaks for a while. The adrenaline leaves its cold on my tongue. Lindsay's hand finds my hand between the seats and stays there, not for comfort but to say we're still in the same weather. How far we have come, I think—how the world has burned the softness out of us, and called it growing up.

Jex breaks the quiet first. "You meant that," he says to Sam, eyes on the road. "About the chip."

Sam doesn't answer right away. He rolls his shoulders as if trying to make them fit. "If it comes to it."

"You fry the IMC with a solar microwave rig," Jex says, thinking out loud the way he does when he sharpens his fear into facts. "You kill the uplink. Maybe it stops the slippage. Maybe it burns the infection out of the current. Maybe it burns you."

"Maybe," Sam says. He takes the corner gentle, not to call attention. "There was a theory on the wire," he adds, and glances at me in the rearview. "Back when we called it that. Standing columnar waves. You set a pulse upright in the field and it holds for a breath too long—like a ripple that forgets to die. Long enough to stop the wrong kind of current."

I don't pretend to know what it means, only that it sounds like a thing that could break the world or mend it.

"In our time," I say, and I can't help myself, "we call it the internet; not very fast."

Sam's mouth does a small thing that, in another life, might be a smile. "Cruder name. Better beer."

Jex snorts. "Beer was better when it went bad quicker."

"Everything was, but I wouldn't know the difference," Lindsay says, and she says it in that wry way she has when truth hurts too much to dress, and it seems Jex brings out the lighter side of Sam when they talk.

We hit the feeder road that runs along the drainage canal and take it north. Water moves under a skin of scum like a thought it doesn't want to say. Towers in the middle distance look like stripped trees. The wind pushes dust across the lanes in low herds.

At the first stop sign that still matters to anyone, Sam does the thing he always does, which is look three ways even when only two exist. Satisfied with every possible past, he drives on.

"Doctor," Sam says finally. The word stays in the car, like we've carried Bresner's ghost out with us. "We owe him more than we can admit."

Jex gives a dry laugh that doesn't reach his eyes. "We owe the whole city, the world." He pauses, shakes his head. "No. Not like that. We owe the one that comes after, if we can save it."

Sam's gaze stays on the road ahead. "We don't trust him," he says. "Can't. Not yet."

Lindsay looks up from the map on her lap. "You think he'll sell us out?"

"I think anyone desperate enough to live will trade anything," Sam says. "Information. People. Doesn't matter."

The silence that follows is sharp. Even the engine seems to listen.

Jex nods slowly. "Then we check it first."

"The dome," Sam says. "Sector Nine. If it's clean, we use it. If it's not, we burn it and find another way."

No one argues. The road unspools beneath us, gray and empty, as if the world itself wants to see whether we mean what we say.

Lindsay leans forward between the seats. "I'm not going home until we save it," she says. She's looking at Sam, but I feel the edge of it too. "Your world. Both of yours. I'm not leaving if there's a chance."

I hear my own voice answer before my mind catches up. "Same."

Sam keeps his eyes on the road. He does not nod. He does not thank us. He lets the air say what he won't: that the car has found a new weight and has balanced it. We are now one team—the burden no longer his alone.

We try the radio, because habit is stronger than instruction, and it gives us a long, dry hiss that pretends to be music. Sam flicks it off with a small motion of his thumb.

"No worries," Jex says, and reaches down into the footwell where he has stowed his bag. He comes up with a brick-colored cassette player scarred by hands that have used it across centuries. He holds it up in the mirror. "What? I like antiques."

Lindsay laughs, a tired, clean sound. "You collect them or they collect you?"

"Bit of both," he says, and snaps the lid open. The cassette inside has a label that looks written on a moving bus. He closes the lid and presses play.

The tape rolls. Static first, then the bass line—steady, patient, like something remembering how to breathe. The drums join after, a heartbeat someone has taught to be brave. A guitar walks in and then tries to leave. A voice carries the world's sorrow but no longer begs it to make sense.

Love, love will tear us apart again...

None of us speaks. The road goes by like dark water under a bridge you don't know you've built. I watch the city in the windows, the way its broken lights try to pretend they're stars if you don't look close.

I think of the lighter in Sam's pocket again, the small truth stamped on its side—*Light 'em if you got 'em*. Some words survive their wars by learning how to laugh at them.

I think of Bresner's trembling hands, the lab still humming with what we've taken, the dome he's named like a promise.

And then the plan itself—spread across that battered table, drawn over with ghosts of older maps: serum, flux weave, and explosives cobbled from kitchen chemicals and false assurances. In the end, a plan is just the story we tell ourselves before the truth arrives.

The tape clicks. Turns itself. The song finds itself again on the other side, as if time learned the trick from plastic long before we ever did. The voice comes back and lies down over the noise of the engine like a tired dog that still knows its name.

We drive past the burned-out factory we lit to get our chance. Smoke writes the sky in the alphabet of endings. The automated firefighting rigs stand in a crooked ring, dead lights like closed eyes. Men with hoses move there instead, arms heavy, water arcing in clumsy parabolas. I feel, briefly, a love for them so sharp it seems a betrayal. They're doing an old thing in a world that has forgotten how. I press my palm to the glass. It's cold.

"Where to lay low," I ask when the road bends toward the hills.

"My uncle's place," Jex says. "He used to run a bait shop out by the irrigation reservoir. Nothing lives there now but spiders and a calendar from a year that didn't end right."

"Perfect," Sam says.

We climb. The city falls behind in scales of gray. The reservoir opens out like a mouth that has bit into sky and kept the taste. The bait shop slouches against a bank of cracked concrete. A torn awning does its best to mean shade.

Jex pulls a key from under a rock stamped with the word *WELCOME* in letters that have never convinced anybody.

Inside smells like dust and line oil and old sunlight. We ghost through the aisles between bins of lures that shine like the eyes of small saints. A map of lakes hangs on the far wall, the paper bubbled and lifted where damp has made its soft argument and won.

We sit on overturned buckets and the counter, each of us choosing silence the way you choose which pain to keep. Jex sets the bag on the counter and takes out what we've come for: the vials, the weave wrapped in dull foil that makes a thin crinkling sound like winter grass.

Sam lays his palms flat beside them and then lifts them again. I see him make the shape of a decision and try not to scare it away.

"We get the cold fusion data," Sam says. His voice carries no weight of hope, only direction. "We deliver it to Bresner ourselves—face to face—and inform him we've secured the cold fusion. He'll know it's waiting at the botanical dome. Then…" He touches the place behind his ear where the IMC is inserted into his brain. "Then I take Lindsay and Markus home. After that, we microwave the chip. We end my link."

"And maybe you," Jex says, because a man like him will always keep you honest.

Sam meets his eyes. "We fix a world and call it even."

Lindsay's voice comes small and sharp from the corner where she's chosen a stool with a cracked blue cushion.

"You're not going to die," she says. She doesn't blink. "Tell me you heard me."

Sam does not look away. "I heard you," he says, and he means both the words and the promise beneath them, which is that he'll do it anyway if it comes to that. The air in the room shifts a little, as if it has leaned in to listen and then changed its mind.

We draw up the pieces: times, routes, aliases to slip through the next set of locks. We mark the path to Sector Nine and the botanical dome—the meeting place, the hand-off, the secret buried under glass and green rot. The cold fusion will wait there, sealed beneath the soil until we tell Bresner where to find it.

We list the points in 1979 that might still hold what the world tried to erase: the *Marigold Array*, yes, but also the university labs that archive copies out of habit, the engineers who think deletion is a crime against progress, and a warehouse in Nevada where forgotten machines go to dream of purpose.

On paper, the plan looks clean—lines crossing like veins, steady and sure. But I know better. Plans like that catch everything except what they're meant to.

Night comes with the sound that always comes here at night: the wind practicing for a storm it won't get right. I look at Lindsay under the hanging light and feel the dangerous peace that visits me in the morning when she sleeps. It's the same peace; we begin in peace, we end in peace, but everything in between is hell.

We sleep in shifts. Sam doesn't sleep at all. I wake once to find him on the steps outside, looking at nothing. The cassette player sits beside him, open to breathe. His hand is in his pocket. I know which pocket.

"I have a thought," I say, just to keep my head clear.

"Bring it here," he says.

"When you said standing columnar waves." I sit. The concrete leaches heat out of my bones. "It sounded like prayer that learned math."

He turns that over and nods. "Or math that learned why prayer was invented."

I nod too, though I don't understand a word of it. The science of what he carries always sounds half like faith, half like failure. I just know it matters—to him, to whatever future he still believes in.

"You're really going to die for it," I say, not a question.

"If the choice is between one man and a world," he says, "it's not a choice."

"Feels like one," I respond.

"It should," he says, and after that he says nothing for a long time. The stars are pale and distant. A satellite drags a crooked line and then loses itself behind cloud. The humming in the wires above us comes and goes like a mood.

We leave before dawn. The car feels smaller, more ours. The cassette player goes into the glove compartment like a small animal that has decided to trust us.

Sector Nine is quiet, the kind of quiet that means no one has worked there in years. We stop near the botanical dome—half collapsed, half standing—its panels fogged with age, its shape still holding to purpose out of habit.

The air is heavy as we approach. The dome's panels are clouded, some shattered inward, others holding light that no longer comes from the sun. Metal vines thread through its frame, brittle with rust.

We find a break in the old security fence and slip through. Inside, the air is warm, humid. A generator somewhere deep in the structure still cycles every few minutes, exhaling a low pulse through the floor. The smell is a mix of wet soil and burnt plastic.

We move in single file. Jex keeps the torch low, the beam carving through dust and hanging pollen. Sam is ahead, quiet, scanning corners and vents, testing each sound as if it can betray us.

"This is it," Jex says, voice just above a whisper.

Sam nods once. "It'll work. Bresner can find the cold fusion here—or finish what he started if he has to. The place was built for it."

Lindsay steps closer, her voice careful. "You think he'd come back here to work? Alone?"

Jex shrugs. "There's an old lab inside, at the center. Climate controls, sealed chamber, still running on auxiliary power. He could rig a workspace out of that easy."

Sam glances up at the faint glow above us. "Then he'll have what he needs."

No one speaks for a while. The dome groans softly in the wind, glass shifting against metal. Water drips from somewhere high, counting the seconds slower than time.

We walk the perimeter once more, marking the exits, the vents, the broken lines of power still humming faintly underfoot.

"Thirty days," Sam says. "Or less."

We leave the dome in silence. Behind us, the structure catches the gray light and holds it—quiet, suspended, like something waiting to wake.

We drive. The city flickers back to life in places, a broken circuit testing itself for power. We see a bus stuck at an angle with no driver. We see a woman sweeping the steps of a building that doesn't deserve it. We see a boy with a kite made from a plastic bag and the bones of an umbrella; the kite flies, because nothing in the world is consistent except refusal.

At the access lane to the North Magway, Sam glances at us in the mirror—Jex, then me, then Lindsay. It isn't a question, just a measure of whether we're still holding together. Whatever he sees, it settles him. He guides the car onto the incline, and we rise into a morning that, for once, doesn't resist.

We do not speak of 1979, though it waits like a place behind a curtain we'll have to walk through. We do not speak of microwave rigs and chips and the shape of a man's life when he has to put it in a furnace and hope the heat leaves the world better. We let the car hold those for us. It does. It's good at holding.

When the road straightens into its long, forgiving line, Jex reaches into the glove box and brings out the cassette player again. No ceremony. He presses play.

The click. The breath. The guitar. The drums that push and pull like a tide with a grudge. The voice that has learned to live inside a wound without making a home of it.

Love, love will tear us apart again…

Lindsay puts her head on my shoulder and watches the road unspool. I watch her reflection in the glass and see the person who has decided to stay in a broken century because someone has asked the world for grace and the world has said, not yet, but if you insist.

We are four people in a car that knows the way a small thing can move against a large one if it doesn't pretend to be bigger than it is. We are armed with stolen science, a doctor's faith, a drop-off location for a cold fusion sample, and a song by men who don't live to see the world they write for. It feels like enough. It feels like nothing. It feels like the truth.

The engine hums and sometimes misses and then remembers itself. The sky opens and then closes. Somewhere behind us a siren tries to decide if it can still mean what it used to mean.

We drive on, toward a year that has already happened for them, toward a city that wants to keep its heart, toward an hour where a man might stand very still inside a column of light and let it burn what needs burning. In the rearview, I see Sam's eyes. They have the calm of a soldier who knows the last bullet has his name on it.

The song finishes and the tape runs past the last of its magnetized story and clicks and keeps turning for a breath, the way time does when it thinks you aren't looking. Then it stops. The wheels on the player slow, and we let the silence take us for a while.

We don't need words. The world says enough for all of us: the hiss of tires, the rattle in the dash, the wind taking its practice runs. Machines breaking down in the distance, yes, and the infection of time running its slow fever through steel and bone. But also the ordinary—Lindsay's hand over mine, Jex counting exits in his head, Sam watching the line and promising the line he'll keep it straight as long as he can.

Morning widens. The car keeps to the center. And the chapter we're inside does what all chapters do if you let them—it carries us forward, breath by breath, until the page turns and we go with it.

Chapter Ten

Year: 2052 — Markus

The bait shop holds its breath the way old rooms do when no one has asked anything of them for years. Dust hangs where sunlight slants through a pane cracked into a spider's patient grammar. A map of lakes, bubbled from heat and time, curls at the edges like it wants to swim off the wall. The generator in the back room complains, coughs, and settles into a hand-cranked hum you can feel in the teeth.

Jex moves through it like someone touching a childhood he doesn't trust to be real—palming the register that still rings, rapping a knuckle on the glass bait case gone dry, straightening the slouch in a stack of foam coolers. "He kept everything," he says, meaning his uncle and meaning himself.

Sam sits at the counter under the nail-hung lures that gleam like patient eyes. His phone lights his face a soft blue; lines drift across it—names, diagrams, failures with dates. He reads quietly, thumb stopping, backing up, moving on. *Marigold Array.* Pre-ban research groups. The old arguments dressed as white papers: not enough containment, too much faith.

Lindsay and I take the high stool near him and set the kit on the counter. Two vials—cold blue when the room goes dim, almost clear when the sun flares. The roll of flux weave looks like dull cloth until you touch it; then it tingles the fingertips and leaves a trace, as if the skin has remembered a fence.

"Faraday weave," I say before I can stop myself. "In my time they'd call it that."

Jex leans in, interested like a cat. "You mean a Faraday cage you can wear."

"Something like that."

"Semantics," he says, but not unkindly. "Names change slower than the world, that's all."

Lindsay runs a finger along the edge of the weave and pulls her hand back like it might bite. "When it's time, who's getting the jab first?" She tries a smile that doesn't quite stay. "I vote you two argue it out."

I laugh because I'm supposed to. The vials make a small
sound when they touch—glass thinking about singing. It
occurs to me how close *precaution* sits to *permission*, how easily
one becomes the other when fear gets a vote.

Sam doesn't look up, but I feel him noticing. There's a way a
man reads when he's also counting the people in the room
by their breaths. He swipes to a page full of densities and
threshold models and lets it go dim again. "Field drift in
twenty-eighty's worse than the models predict," he says to
the counter. "Whatever we do, we do it fast."

Jex goes to the door. Outside, the lake wears a mild color. A
light machine—the jet-ski—bobbles at a post, rope looping
it to the world with more faith than knots deserve. "He left
the toys, too," he says. "The coastal types call it a water glide.
Here it's just a loud way to make the afternoon shorter."

Sam comes to stand beside him. He doesn't hurry his looks;
he lets the scene come to him. The jet-ski knocks once
against the post, like it wants in. He turns to me. "Take her
out," he says. "While the day still wants you."

Lindsay is already moving. She runs through the doorway,
hair snatching at the light, and the shop feels larger for the
space she leaves behind. I follow, but Sam's hand finds my
shoulder before the threshold. He presses once—steady, not
heavy.

"Enjoy it," he says. "You don't know which tomorrows
belong to you."

It isn't advice so much as permission, and it lifts something
in me I hadn't known I'm carrying. I nod and go.

The lake takes the jet-ski like it's been waiting. Lindsay straddles the seat and grins at me over her shoulder, both hands on the grips like the machine is a horse with opinions. I climb on, and the hull settles into our weight. She leans back into me just enough to make breathing different. I squeeze the throttle and the shore slips; the water opens where we ask it to, clean V writing behind us, a minor hymn.

From the bait shop porch, two figures watch—Jex with hands in pockets, Sam with one on the post as if he can keep the day upright. The wind off the water smells faintly of iron and something sweet that might be rotten apples far upwind. The motor's pitch rises and falls; Lindsay's laugh carries, breaks, carries again.

We keep to the long side of the reservoir, where cattails make a thin army and dragonflies cast tiny zippers over the skin of the water. She turns her head so I can hear. "Feels like cheating."

"What does?"

"Being happy here."

I don't have an answer that wouldn't make more promises than we own. I ease off and let the machine idle. The ripples go out and come back and touch us with our own making. The jet-ski engine answers itself with a higher note. We cut across the lake in a long arc toward them. Jex cups his hands and shouts, "We're fishing! You're scaring the smart ones and teaching the dumb ones to hide!"

I turn quick and spray a curtain of water that doesn't quite reach them. "You're welcome!" Lindsay yells, delighted to be the villain.

Sam puts two fingers to his temple like he might reset into another hour just to make a point. "Don't tempt me," he calls, and his voice carries the grin his mouth doesn't show.

We idle into the shallows, cut the engine, and slide off. The water is cleaner than the year deserves—cool along the shins, a shock that makes the skin wake. Lindsay wades out deeper, then dives in a smooth line and comes up laughing, her hair flat and dark. She waves without words and turns onto her back to float. The sky holds her like it knows how. I join Sam and Jex to let Lindsay have her time in the sun as the water holds her shape.

Jex hands me his spare rod. "You fish or just stand near the idea of it?"

"I can learn to insult the water," I say, sounding like Jex.

"That's all fishing is," he says, approving.

Sam sets the tackle box between us and sits with his forearms on his knees, the posture of a man willing to be still. The float bobs once, twice, then chooses a direction I'm not ready for. I jerk. The line comes up empty and light. Jex makes a noise that means: lesson.

Jex bumps his shoulder against Sam's like men do when they're not sure the moment needs words. "Matchmaker," he says, smiling into the lake and toward me.

"If I believe in anything," Sam says, "it's love that outlives its calendar."

Jex sniffs, pleased and annoyed. "You'll have them thanking you or cursing you by nightfall."

"They already do," Sam says, and lets himself almost smile as he glances at me.

They start talking in the plain way men talk when the subject turns to what is owed and who can stand where. Jex will stay. The ghost town has cabins enough to lose himself in and food enough to turn patience into practice. "Plenty of cans," he says. "Plenty of hooks. I'll be here when you blink back with the past in your pocket."

"Tomorrow," Sam says. He keeps his eyes on the line where dark water runs deeper. "They need a day before the slip."

Jex nods like someone agreeing with weather. "Then I'll make a night of it. There's a freezer that still holds its tongue; I'll see what it's been saving. We'll call it a barbecue if the charcoal remembers how to be char."

We talk about most things and nothing. They tell pieces of their twenties, which are louder and closer to fire than mine. I tell them I envy whatever version of youth lets you mistake noise for meaning. Jex returns serve: "Says the boy from nineteen-ninety-nine. Add up the arithmetic—you're older than me by different math."

I take the joke and laugh as instructed. It's an easy afternoon; even our griefs wear plain clothes.

Jex, who never leaves a silence unfed, says Juliette's name the way you drop a stone in shallow water to see where the ripples find shore. Sam doesn't flinch. "I keep her," he says. No flourish. "Some days I keep her harder."

"What do you love to do with her?" Jex asks, trying to be kind by pretending it's a casual question.

Sam thinks, then lets the answer out like it's been waiting by the door. "Haiku," he says. "Back and forth through the chip. You think the line and it arrives as a whisper where she is. No typing. Just the words. Sometimes you hear yourself better when you don't use your mouth."

He takes a folded slip from his pocket. Paper in this century feels like a confession. He smooths it on his knee and reads, not looking at us but not alone either:

Seasons forget us.
But love keeps its own calendar.
Time learns it from you.

Jex says, "She'll hear that. When we fix it."

Sam folds the paper exactly in thirds. "Maybe," he says, and stands up to make the air lighter. "Now—somebody has to prove mastery over charcoal. Watch me fail."

"Careful," Jex says, rising too. "It takes a real man to ruin meat correctly."

"That's why I asked you to watch," Sam says, and walks toward the cabins with the look of a person willing to wrestle a simple thing and lose.

They go off together, arguing about airflow like it has wronged them in a past life. I stay on the bank and manage to pretend I know where fish prefer to be unseen. Lindsay's laugh floats in from somewhere midway across the lake, then the water takes it and gives back the hum of the generator, the smallest sound of a town remembering its name.

I watch her cut a slow line toward shore, the rhythm unhurried, the body sure. It hits me then with the clean pain of a simple truth: a good day is not a promise; it is proof that promises once existed. I reel in and set the rod down before I start believing I can hold anything in place by gripping it.

Behind me, Jex shouts something about tinder and dignity. Sam answers with something about vents and last chances. The smell of smoke arrives, thin at first, then real. Somewhere a freezer door thunks open and a man discovers whatever the past has kept cold for him. The lake puts a small wind in my face. If I close my eyes I can inventory the scene by sound alone—the slip of water on stone, the line's faint whistle in air, two men pretending the world will wait until the coals are ready.

I open them. Lindsay raises a hand, palm bright with water, and I raise mine back. It feels like agreeing with the day.

By the time the smoke turns the sky the color of copper, the grill is alive and arguing. Jex has found half a bag of charcoal, three questionable cans, and something wrapped in foil that turns out to be mashed potatoes. Sam takes charge of the fire with a seriousness that makes me smile.

Lindsay and I sit nearby, still damp from earlier, the air cool on our skin. She's changed into one of Jex's flannels, sleeves rolled twice at the wrists, hair loose and drying in waves. She looks calm in the kind of way that makes time hesitate.

"Think they know what they're doing?" she asks, nodding at the two of them by the grill.

"They think they do," I say. "That's enough to start a religion."

She laughs softly. The sound breaks something open in me I hadn't realized is locked. The kind of sound you remember in rooms years later.

The sky dims to that late color where the day forgets itself. The air fills with the smell of fish, yams, something almost edible. Sam pokes at the food, Jex gives instructions that make no sense, and somehow it all works.

When Jex finally shouts, "Dinner!" it sounds like victory.

We sit in a half-circle around the grill—Sam, Jex, Lindsay, me—plates full of mismatched food. Fish beside cheeseburgers, corn beside raisins. It shouldn't work, but it does.

"This feels like Thanksgiving," I say, grinning.

"What's that?" Sam asks without looking up.

I meet Lindsay's eyes, and we both say, "Never mind."

Later, the plates are empty and the night comes down soft and full. The fire turns into a heartbeat of orange. Lindsay leans close, whispering something I don't catch at first.

"What?" I ask.

She shakes her head. "Nothing. Just thinking how strange it is—how we're here, now. The year, the world, all of it."

"Yeah," I say. "It's almost peaceful. That's what scares me."

She turns then, really turns, and the quiet stretches between us like a bridge. I say her name and she stops breathing for half a second. I step closer. She meets me halfway.

The kiss isn't hesitant this time. It's a small surrender that feels earned. Then another, deeper, until the air around us seems to slow down. We break apart for a second, eyes searching, and then we find each other again.

"I was wondering when you'd finally do that," she says, voice barely above a breath.

Before I can answer, we hear clapping from the fire. Jex, of course. Sam joins with one slow clap just to make it worse. Lindsay laughs into my shoulder.

We walk back toward the cabins together, hand in hand. Jex tosses me a key on a loop of string.

"Cabin forty-two," he says. "*Cosmos in Heaven.* Sheets are only halfway haunted."

Sam says, "Get some sleep. Tomorrow we start new work."

We walk the path to our cabin under a broken moon. Inside smells like cedar and a long-ago summer. The mattress sighs the way old things do when they're relieved to be used.

Lindsay stands in the middle of the room, hair still damp, shirt clinging where the lake hasn't quite let go. I say her name and she turns. That's enough. I step in and kiss her once, soft, testing the room we've built between us these past days. She catches my shirt and pulls me closer.

"Finally," she says against my mouth, and then there isn't much talking. The second kiss is not polite. It has the truth of every almost that comes before it. We press into each other like a decision made at last. When we break, it's only to breathe and look—quick, startled, glad—and then we find each other again, slower this time, closer.

Somewhere outside, Jex whoops and claps, and Sam adds a single dry cheer that makes us laugh without stopping. We keep our foreheads touching until the laughter dies back to the fire's small sounds.

We don't rush the rest. We let the room be a room. Hands, warmth, the simple fact of being held. If the world wants to tilt, it can do it without us for a while. What happens after that isn't for the world to know, only to remember.

We fall asleep late, tangled and tired in the good way, the lake moving the moon across the curtain like a small white boat.

Morning comes as if it has been waiting just outside the door. Sam and Jex are already up—Sam in plain clothes that pass for ordinary, his bag heavier than it looks; Jex prowling the roofline, talking about antennas and signal ghosts like he can coach an old mast into listening across time. Coffee steams in metal cups. Lindsay presses one into my hands and her fingers stay a moment longer than they need to.

"Today," Sam says, and doesn't add anything to it. He doesn't have to.

I look at Lindsay and feel the old fear try the lock—losing this, losing her—but it doesn't open. Not today. I kiss her temple and taste the lake still there, faint as a memory.

We step outside together. The day is clean and thin, the kind that makes everything seem more temporary. Jex is already pacing by the old antenna mast, tapping at its rusted joints with a wrench like it might answer back.

"I've been thinking," he says. "If I can tune the mast to a narrow band to my IMC, I might piggyback off your IMC frequency. Direct link. Real-time."

Sam smiles faintly. "Different worlds, Jex. Different frequencies."

Jex waves the wrench like a flag of persistence. "Yeah, but physics has a soft spot for stubborn men. I'll argue with it until it takes a nap."

Sam just shakes his head, amused, and the light off the lake catches in his eyes for a moment before he looks away.

When Lindsay and I turn toward the coffee, I feel Sam's hand land on my shoulder. I stop. He doesn't squeeze. He just rests it there a second, like a vote of confidence.

"Enjoy it," he says. "You never know about tomorrow."

"I'm trying," I say.

"Good," he says, and lets me go.

The air outside carries that early light that makes the world look newly washed, as if the colors have agreed to be honest for a moment. Sam checks his bag again with the calm precision of someone who understands that even small adjustments can shape an entire future. Lindsay moves beside me, her coffee already finished, her expression balanced between acceptance and something softer, something close to reluctance.

"Coordinates are stable," Sam says. His tone is quiet, almost formal. "We should land close to this place, but earlier. Don't expect landmarks. Don't expect time to be consistent."

Jex stands under the antenna mast, still adjusting the receiver coil as though it might answer questions he isn't ready to voice. "If this thing whispers back," he says, "we'll know the link held. If it stays silent, I'll assume you're too busy in the past to bother with me."

Sam offers a small, almost invisible smile at that, though it holds no humor.

We come together in a loose and uncertain circle. Lindsay's hand slides into mine, gentle but firm, grounding me in a moment that feels strangely delicate. The generator hums behind us, the lake holds itself in stillness, and even the birds seem unwilling to interrupt what is about to happen.

"Are we ready?" Sam asks.

No one agrees aloud, but no one steps back.

He taps the side of his phone, and I wonder—briefly, foolishly—what that moment feels like inside his skull. The IMC chip must awaken in its own way, humming or warming or whispering its unfamiliar electricity into the bone.

The air folds. Light washes out the world in a single, fierce breath.

When the brightness falls away, everything has changed.

The lake is gone.
The bait shop is gone.

Year — 1979

Nothing stands except open earth, bright and clean, as if the land has just risen from sleep. The ground beneath our feet smells of clay holding the memory of rain. We stand in the space where the building will one day exist, except here it is only possibility—an outline waiting for time to draw it in.

Lindsay turns slowly, as though afraid to disturb the silence. "It feels like arriving before the story learns how to begin."

Sam checks the phone again, his eyes moving over data that barely recognizes itself. "1979," he says quietly. "Give or take a few hours."

The stillness is different here—wide, unhurried, unobserved. No drones above us, no electrical pressure humming along the air, no hidden circuitry embedded in the wind. Just sky

and soil and the kind of emptiness that makes the future feel
imaginative rather than inevitable.

We follow a thin dirt path that will one day become the road
leading to the cabins. Mesquite trees scratch lightly at the
horizon. Dry grass brushes our ankles. A forgotten billboard
lies half-sunk in the sand, its paint flaked by the sun: *Kasper
Lake Resort — Coming Soon.*

Sam pauses when he sees it, his expression unreadable.

"You've done this before," I say. "Does it ever feel normal?"

He shakes his head. "Time doesn't become easier," he says.
"You just learn to stop pretending it cares what you want."

We reach a service road, cracked and tired but still clinging
to purpose. A rusted truck sits crooked in the weeds, the
keys resting in the ignition like the world has placed them
there for us alone.

Sam turns the key. The truck coughs once, then settles into a
rough, determined idle.

"Our transportation," he says softly.

Lindsay climbs in first, sunlight slipping through her hair in
thin golden strands. I follow, still feeling the quiet tremor the
time lapse has left inside my bones. Sam drives without
looking back. Dust rises behind us in a thin, wandering trail,
as if marking the boundary between two different versions
of the same world.

The highway opens in front of us like something unfinished—long, pale, and honest about how far we still have to go. The world in 1979 feels wider than ours, younger in a way that makes my chest tighten. Too many colors. Too much sky. No hum in the air. No drifting static pressing at the nerves. Just wind and heat and the low drone of Sam's found-in-the-weeds truck.

Lindsay leans her head against the passenger window, watching the land pass like it's a story she's almost heard before. Sam drives with both hands on the wheel, shoulders squared, alert in that way he gets when the world is too quiet for his liking.

"Feels wrong without the grid noise," he says, barely above the engine.

"What?" I ask.

"That," he says, tapping the dashboard. "Silence. It's suspicious."

I laugh, mostly because I need to. "People used to call this normal."

"People used to drink water from hoses," Sam says. "I try not to think about it."

Lindsay smiles at that. Even in another century, she finds small reasons to be amused. It makes the world seem less breakable.

We hit the interstate after an hour of dirt roads. Sam merges like he's done it a thousand times, although I know he hasn't.

Cars move past us—bright colors, clean lines, people inside unaware of anything beyond their day. A man sipping from a travel mug. A kid asleep with a stuffed dinosaur. A woman singing with her whole face.

The normalcy is almost violent.

"They have no idea," Lindsay whispers.

Sam doesn't answer. He doesn't have to. He keeps his eyes forward, scanning the miles like they're a code only he can read.

The First Two Hundred Miles

We stop in a town that still thinks gas is cheap. Sam fills the tank while Lindsay and I stand under a sun that feels too warm for November.

"I could stay in this year," Lindsay says quietly.

"You could," I say. "But you won't."

She nudges my arm. "You're right. I trust Sam. And you."

Trust. I swallow it like something too big to chew.

We grab water and chips from a convenience store that smells like citrus cleaner and old newsprint. The cashier doesn't look at us twice. It feels like getting away with something.

Five Hundred Miles In

The land changes. Mountains rise like old bones. The road curves through them in long, thoughtful bends. I take the wheel while Sam sleeps in the passenger seat, head tilted back, one hand on his bag even in unconsciousness.

Lindsay watches him. "He doesn't rest," she says.

"He thinks rest will cost us time."

"Maybe it will," she says. "But maybe not resting will cost him more."

She doesn't say the other part: *And I don't want to lose him.*

We stop near an overlook. Lindsay climbs a short slope and stands there with the wind in her hair, looking at a world she has never been meant to see. Sam focuses on vehicle movement.

"You okay?" I ask.

She nods. "I just… it's strange. Everything feels too real here. Like the world hasn't broken yet."

"It hasn't," I say. "Not for another thirty-two years."

She takes my hand. "Then let's give it a fighting chance."

Nine Hundred Miles In

Night finds us somewhere outside Flagstaff. Pines crowd the road, black and watchful, their tops catching the moon like thin knives. The town is small but restless—gas stations still open, diners still humming, headlights drifting like slow questions.

Sam wakes up, stretches, and takes the wheel without a word. He drives for a few minutes, rolling his shoulders, settling into the night.

"You ever been through here?" he asks.

"No," I say.

"Same," he mutters. "Feels like a place that keeps its own secrets."

Lindsay smiles, the soft kind that comes from something only she notices. "Better than the cities," she says. "At least here, nothing's pretending."

Sam huffs. "Pretending's harmless. It's the believing that gets people. Folks think time owes them clarity. It doesn't. Time lends. Then it takes back with interest."

He says it offhand, but it sticks in my ribs like a nail someone doesn't bother pulling out; lodged somewhere deep.

The Last Stretch

The facility is still three hundred miles away—a private research complex with polite fences and impolite security. We check into a roadside motel with buzzing lights and a carpet that has fought one too many wars.

Sam spreads the printed schematics on the bed. The blue feels too bright under the yellow lamp.

"We need three days," he says. "One day to watch, one day to test, one day to act."

"Act how?" Lindsay asks.

Sam traces a path with his finger. "Carefully."

I lean over the map. "And if they catch us?"

Sam doesn't hesitate. "They won't."

He believes it. Or he needs us to believe it.

The next two weeks are a blur of attempts that die too soon:

– A wrong turn that leads to a guard checkpoint.
– A camera we haven't seen.
– A technician who comes back from lunch early.
– A failed badge clone.
– A shadow moving where no shadow should be.

Each time Sam pulls out the phone.
Each time the world folds.
Each time we reset to the morning before.

Time travel isn't a thrill. It's erosion. I feel pieces of myself get left behind—seconds, thoughts, versions of me that learn something the others don't.

After the tenth reset, Lindsay cries quietly in the motel bathroom, thinking we can't hear. I stand outside the door and don't know how to fix anything.

After the fifteenth reset, Sam's hands shake for the first time.

After the nineteenth, we finally find the rhythm.

"Clockwork," I say.

Sam nods. "Now we move."

Everything clicks:

– The guard at the north gate always checks his phone at 07:43.
– The security camera loops every twelve minutes.
– The ID badge of the man in the red jacket works on the door to Lab C.
– Lab C has a secondary door with no alarm—painted shut, but not locked.
– The cold fusion archive is in a vault behind a wall that looks like any other wall.

We move like we've been born for it.

Sam bypasses the first lock.
Lindsay stands lookout.
I keep my hand on the charge Jex makes.

We find the data drives—black, neatly labeled, humming faintly.
We find the core sample—sealed, smaller than my hand, a

dull metallic cylinder that feels heavier than physics means it to be.

Sam holds it up. "This is it."

The cold fusion core rests in his palm, humming faintly, as if it recognizes where it's been taken. A small sun stolen from tomorrow.

I don't breathe until we're outside.

The drive back is fast, frantic, silent. Tires ripping over asphalt. Lindsay's hands tremble in her lap. No one speaks. Not even Sam. The sky grows darker with every mile we put behind us, clouds folding in like something alive.

As we near the empty plot where the bait shop will someday stand, I see movement above — a helicopter, blacked out, no lights. Just a silhouette carving the night.

Lindsay whispers, "Sam…"

Headlights bloom behind us. One. Two. Three. SUVs swallowing the road. Brakes scream. Doors slam. Gravel scatters as men in dark suits step forward, rifles already lifted, trained on us like judgment.

A voice detonates through a megaphone.
"Put the objects on the ground and step away from the vehicle. This is your only warning."

Sam doesn't move.
He looks at me once. Steady. Certain.

Then his thumb taps the screen.

The first shot cracks the air open.

Glass explodes. Metal shrieks. The windshield spiders outward as another round tears through the hood. Lindsay screams. The world becomes sound and heat and panic.

Sam presses reset.

More gunfire. A storm of it. Muzzles flashing like malignant stars. Bullets slicing through the second before it ends.

And then the world rips apart.

Light — violent, consuming — floods everything. The sound of rifles stretches and warps, pulled thin as time collapses inward. My stomach drops. Reality dissolves. Space folds like wet paper.

And then—

2080.

Silence.

The bait shop stands where dust once lived. A tired structure beneath a washed-out sky. The air looks older. Heavier. Like it remembers everything.

Jex stands a few feet away, frozen, breath caught in his throat.
"You're back," he says, disbelief and relief breaking together. "And you've got it."

Sam opens his hand.

The cold fusion core gleams there — flawless, impossible —
a captured star ripped from the spine of time.

No one speaks.

Because the echoes of gunfire are still in our bones.

And we all understand it now.

We didn't just escape.

We outran death by a single heartbeat.

Chapter Eleven

Year: 2080 — Markus

Something feels wrong before I even look down. Not pain—not yet. More like the memory of heat, or the ghost of someone brushing past you in a dark hallway.

The rift always leaves a shiver in my bones, but this is different. Sharper.

Lindsay reaches me first.

"Markus—wait."

She grabs my arm to steady me, and her palm slides across my side.

Her hand comes away red.

She stares at it like the color can't possibly belong to this quiet morning.

"Markus—you're bleeding."

My stomach drops. My ribs tighten. Only then does the burn spread itself across the skin, full and bright.

"It's nothing," I say automatically. "Just a graze."

But the tremor in my voice betrays me.

Sam is beside me before I even register him moving. He scans me with a look that has nothing to do with the wound and everything to do with guilt.

"Let me see."

I lift my shirt.

A thin, angry line cuts under my ribs—a bullet's whisper. Shallow, but bleeding freely.

Sam's jaw sets—not in anger.

In self-blame.

He doesn't move for a moment. He just stares at that line of blood like it's a sentence written in bad handwriting and he's trying to translate it before it disappears.

Something closes in his face—tight, decisive, familiar. The look of a man who has already made a choice he doesn't want to speak aloud.

"You're not supposed to be touched by any of this," he says quietly.

Jex curses and sprints for supplies. Lindsay presses her sleeve against the wound, her breath shaking.

"It's really not bad," I try again.

Sam shakes his head once. Slow. Final.

"It's enough."

And the way he says it isn't about the bullet.

It's about his decision.

The one he has been trying not to make since the moment we met.

Lindsay's sleeve is already soaked through, a dark bloom spreading across the fabric. Jex comes barreling back with a metal case under his arm—half medical kit, half toolbox. He drops to his knees beside us, swearing under his breath.

"Hold still," he says, which would be funny if not for the way his hands shake.

Sam doesn't kneel. He crouches—back straight, shoulders set, the way someone does when stillness is the only thing keeping them from breaking.

Jex peels my shirt higher. "Bullet grazed you," he mutters. "Clean line, no fragment. Lucky."

Sam flinches at the word *lucky*. I feel it more than see it.

Jex dabs something that stings sharp enough to make my teeth clench. Lindsay holds my arm, her jaw tight, eyes shining like she wishes she can take the pain for me.

But Sam just watches.

Silent.

Thinking.

Making decisions in that head of his like someone loading stones into a bag he plans to carry alone.

When the bleeding slows and Jex wraps the bandage tight, Sam finally speaks.

"We're done here."

Jex looks up. "What do you mean *done*?"

Sam's eyes flick to me, then Lindsay, then the lake. They hold a calm so steady it scares me more than the gunfire did.

"I'm taking them home," he says.

Lindsay freezes. I feel her breath catch.

"Sam—" I start, but he cuts me off with a glance, not harsh, just firm.

"You were grazed," he says. "Next time, maybe it won't be a graze. I'm not risking either of you. Not for this."

Jex exhales through his nose. "Sam, they agreed—"

"And I didn't," Sam says. His voice isn't loud, but the decision inside it is. "This is my mess. My storm. My time. You two were dragged along because of a tether I never meant to create."

Lindsay moves closer, her hand finding his sleeve. "We chose to stay with you."

Sam pulls his arm back—not cruelly, but like someone removing a knife from a wound. "You shouldn't have had to choose at all."

Jex stands, dusting off his hands. "This isn't the place to argue. We need to move. Bresner's waiting."

Sam nods once, the matter closed for him even if it isn't for us.

"Get the suitcase," he says. "We can't risk the core getting jarred."

The cold fusion sample rests inside a small hard-shell case we pad with sweaters, towels, anything soft we can find. The sphere inside hums faintly through the insulation—too quiet for human ears, too loud for human nerves.

Sam lifts it like it's something alive.

"Let's go."

He leads us toward the 2080 *Crawler*, still parked under the pines where we left it before traveling to 1979. Its adaptive metal skin blends into the shade, humming quietly as it registers our proximity. The side door slides open with a soft exhale.

We board without speaking.

Jex drives, fingers tapping calculations on the dash. Sam sits in the back, case between his boots, eyes fixed on the road ahead. Lindsay presses her knee against mine, grounding me despite the sting radiating across my ribcage.

No one says it aloud, but we all feel it:

Something has changed.

Sam is already separating himself from us.

We leave the bait shop at a slow pace, the morning still fragile around us. My ribs pulse in dull waves, but it's the silence between the four of us that hurts worse. Lindsay leans close, her shoulder brushing mine. Jex drives on, muttering to himself about coordinates and field interference. Sam holding the case, eyes forward, jaw carved from stone.

We take the ridge trail—the one that winds above the lake and cuts into a narrow slot between the hills. Sam insists we stay high. "Less chance of watchers," he says.

Jex scoffs. "After what we pulled? Anyone watching already knows."

Sam doesn't respond. He just keeps looking straight.

Half an hour in, Jex stops at an outcrop and motions us down. "We're here."

It doesn't look like a lab.

Just a cliff face with a rusted ventilation lift. Link cables tangling like Christmas lights. Jex pulls them aside, revealing a keypad hidden beneath years of dust.

He punches in a code as he glances back and forth on his portable.

The grate groans open into the bionic dome.

Inside is a narrow hallway, dark but dry, the walls carved rough and unfinished. The air smells of old marble and older secrets.

"Dr. Bresner?" Sam calls.

A voice echoes back, thin but unmistakably human.

"Bring it in, Samuel."

We follow the sound.

The tunnel widens into a chamber with steel tables, battery packs, holographic screens flickering low blue. A man stands near the far bench—older, gray in the beard, eyes bright with the kind of intelligence that never tires itself out.

Dr. Bresner.

He takes one look at the suitcase and exhales like a man watching a miracle arrive.

"You did it," he whispers. "You actually... Sam, you brought me the future."

Sam sets the case on the table and opens it.

Blue light breathes across the room.

Bresner steps forward, reverent as a priest before an altar. "The core... intact. Perfect. And the data?"

Sam hands him the drive.

Bresner almost laughs. "This—this cuts decades. Maybe saves us in time."

Then he stares at Jex, eyes softening.

"Titor," Bresner says warmly. "Good to see you again."

Jex chuckles, rubbing the back of his neck. "Wish I could say the same about me."

Bresner places a hand on his shoulder. "You staying?"

Jex looks at Sam, then at me and Lindsay.

"Yes," he says. "I think I am."

Lindsay's breath curls inward. "Jex…"

He hugs her first—tight, like he doesn't trust any world to let him do it twice.

Then me.

"Look out for each other," he says, gripping my shoulder. "And listen to Sam. He's stubborn, but he's right more often than you think."

Sam doesn't step forward, but something in his expression shifts—softer, almost grateful.

Not farewell. Just acknowledgment.

"We'll be back soon," he says.

Not a promise—Sam never over-promises—but a statement he intends to make true.

Jex grins. "Yeah. I know. Just another hour for me anyway."

He turns back to Bresner and the glowing core.

Sam motions to us. "Come on. We're leaving."

Outside, the wind carries a colder bite—like the world knows a part of our circle has broken off.

Lindsay walks beside Sam. "You're really taking us home."

"I am," Sam says.

"And you're staying here to finish the fight."

He doesn't answer.

He doesn't need to.

That's when I know the decision isn't about strategy or safety.

It's about burden.

About loneliness wearing the shape of duty.

About a man convinced he's the only one who deserves to carry the weight.

But he's wrong.

And none of us can say it in time.

We leave Bresner's lab in silence, the *Crawler* humming low beneath us as it carries us back toward the bait shop. Jex's absence sits in the seats like a fourth body. Lindsay rests her head against the window, eyes distant, hands uneasy in her lap. Sam stares straight ahead, jaw tight, as if he's afraid any expression might weaken his resolve.

The closer we get to the lake, the more I feel the hours slipping through us.

The bait shop looks the same from the outside—old wood, crooked porch, stillness hanging in the beams like dust—but everything inside has changed. Sam walks in first, goes straight behind the counter, and pulls out the military bag he hid days earlier. I recognize the shape before he even unzips it:

—two vials
—one flux weave
—two futures

He doesn't say anything while he checks the contents. Just breathes once—the kind of breath you take when you already know what you have to do.

When he steps back outside, he stops.

Lindsay is holding me. Not lightly. Not politely. Not the way people hold each other when there's time to spare—but the way you cling when the clock is louder than the heartbeat in your throat. Her face is buried against my shirt; my hands are on her back, memorizing the shape of her before the world takes it away again.

Sam doesn't interrupt.

He just slows his steps, giving the moment space. Giving *us* space.

Then he clears his throat—softly, apologetically—and we know it's time.

We stand in a small circle at the edge of the porch, nothing between us and the quiet lake but the truth of what is about to happen.

"You ready?" Sam asks Lindsay.

She nods, though her voice is gone.

Her hand finds mine.

Her other finds Sam's sleeve.

"Take me home," she whispers.

Sam raises the device. The air folds.

Light swallows the lake, the trees, the world.

And then—

1999.

Her world. As if Sam's IMC chip understands intent, as I assumed. No doubt Sam realizes it too.

The sound hits me first—birds, real birds, not drones. Then the smell—fresh soil, cut grass, the trace of laundry drying somewhere downwind. We stand on a quiet residential street.

A few houses, all lived-in. All warm. All normal—but not quite. I can see a faint hint of the sky anomaly creeping in.

Lindsay looks around like she's afraid to breathe.

"Sam…" she whispers.

He points gently.

Her house.

The same one she described in pieces. Porch with chipped yellow paint. Wind chime shaped like a crescent moon. Garden beds she helps her grandparents weed on Saturdays.

And there—just past the fence—her grandparents.

Alive.

Her grandmother kneels in the dirt, hands deep in soil, humming to herself. Her grandfather stands beside her, trimming a rosebush, pausing every now and then to say something that makes her laugh.

Lindsay makes a sound I'll never forget—a half-breath, half-cry, like someone being returned to the universe after being lost between its pages.

She steps forward but stops herself.

Her hands fly to her mouth.

Tears blur her eyes.

"I can't believe… I can't…" She shakes her head. "I thought I'd never see them again."

Her shoulders tremble.

I can't breathe.

Sam steps to her side. Not touching her—just standing there, the way a person stands with someone who is witnessing a miracle they can't hold alone.

"You have to stay hidden," he says softly. "Once you're anchored, you'll step back into their lives like you never left."

She nods, wiping her tears with the heel of her hand.

Then she turns to me.

"Markus…"

My whole chest tightens.

She grabs my face between both hands—desperate, searching, like she's trying to memorize every feature before time erases the edges.

"You saved me," she says. "In more ways than one."

"No," I whisper. "You saved me."

She kisses me then—slow, breaking, final.

A kiss that feels like the end of something I'll spend a lifetime trying to name.

When she pulls back, she rests her forehead to mine for a moment that hurts in every direction.

"I'll look for you," she says.

"And I'll look for you."

Her voice cracks. "Tell me you'll be okay."

"I'll try," I say. The only honest answer I have.

She turns to Sam next.

And the way she looks at him—God—there's gratitude and sorrow and anger and forgiveness all braided together.

"Stay alive," she tells him. "Stay alive and save us."

It isn't a request.

It's a command.

Sam swallows once. "You too."

Lindsay wipes her face, exhales, rolls up her sleeve. Sam hands her the serum. She doesn't hesitate—just plunges the needle into her arm, breath catching as the chemical anchors her.

Then she wraps herself in the flux weave. The fabric glows faintly as it synchronizes with her timeline—and then it disintegrates, golden particles shimmering off her skin. The flux weave fails surviving the time cross. We stand in silence.

Lindsay nods at Sam, giving him the go-ahead to keep going. Everything feels so fast.

She looks at both of us one last time.

"I love you," she says—

to both of us

in different ways

with different meanings

that are both true.

And then—

She walks to her grandparents.

Into her yard.

Into her home.

Into her life.

Sam touches the device and I shout.

"I love you!"

The world cracks open.

And when the light closes—

She is gone.

And it has worked.

Lindsay stays anchored in 1999.

Sam and I stand alone on the same street, the same day—but several hours later. Enough to keep the paradox intact. Enough to confirm she has stayed.

My chest hurts.

Not from the bullet.

From everything else.

I utter a cry so strange that I scare myself.

Sam looks at the empty space where she has been, then at me—looking at me as if he understands my pain. Sam is probably the one person who can understand better than anyone.

The street feels too wide without her. Too quiet.

The air still holds the shape of where she stood, like the world isn't ready to admit she's gone.

My knees feel weak.

Not collapsing—just unsteady, the way a person stands after losing something they didn't know was holding them up. I press a hand to my ribs, not for the wound, but because everything inside me feels suddenly hollow.

"I didn't think it would hurt like this," I say.

The words slip out before I can catch them.

Sam doesn't answer right away.

He just breathes once, slow, steady, the kind of breath you take when you're holding yourself together for someone else.

"It always hurts," he finally says. "When someone goes home without you."

His voice isn't sharp.

It isn't distant.

It's quiet in the way truth is quiet.

My throat tightens.

I look at the house again—her house—the porch, the wind chime, the life she is stepping back into. A life that doesn't have room for me. A life I will never fit into, no matter how many timelines exist.

"She deserved it," I whisper. "All of it. Her home. Her family. Her life back."

Sam nods. "She did."

"But…" The word breaks in my mouth. "It feels like I'm missing a piece of myself."

For the first time since we landed, Sam turns fully toward me.

His eyes are softer than I've ever seen them.

"That's because you are," he says. "But the piece isn't lost. It's just… somewhere you can't reach yet."

A tear slides down my cheek without my permission.

I wipe it away fast, embarrassed, angry at myself for it—but more angry at the universe for making the moment feel like a punishment.

Sam doesn't look away.

He doesn't judge me.

He doesn't expect me to be stronger than I am.

"You're allowed to feel it," he says. "She mattered."

I nod, swallowing hard.

"And so do you," Sam adds.

That's the part that undoes me.

The part that makes the breath shake out of my chest.

The part that makes my vision blur all over again.

Because no one has ever said it like that before.

Not with certainty.

Not like it's something I deserve to hear.

I let out another broken sound—half-sob, half-exhale—and Sam steps closer, not touching me, but standing near enough that I don't feel alone on that quiet street where the past and future have just split us apart.

For a moment, neither of us speaks.

We just stand there, two people holding the same invisible wound.

Then Sam finally says, gently:

"We have one more stop to make."

People begin stepping out of Lindsay's house.

Not her grandparents this time.

Not the two figures we saw tending the garden.

A different couple.

Different faces.

Different lives.

Because this isn't her world.

And she is never meant to exist in mine.

One of them spots us—Sam and me standing in the middle of the street—

but they don't recognize Lindsay because there is no Lindsay here.

Not in this reality.

Not in this version of 1999.

My chest tightens all over again.

I turn away from the house before the grief can catch up to me.

"Let's go find my Aunt Carol," I say.

Sam nods, falling into step beside me.

We walk down the quiet road, past the lawns, past the mailboxes with names I don't know, toward the subdivision where my world cracked open once.

The sky shifts as we walk—those same strange colors, the same shimmer bleeding across the clouds.

My stomach drops.

"It's today," I say, barely a whisper.

The day everything goes wrong.

The day the fracture starts eating through the sky like rot.

Sam slows beside me.

"We can travel back a few days," he says. "Put you somewhere safer. Somewhere before all this hits."

I shake my head immediately.

"No. I don't want to. I want to stay here. In this time. Even if it's broken."

Sam watches me for a long moment, weighing something heavy.

"I'll fix it," he says finally.

Quiet.

Absolute.

Like he isn't making a promise—

but stating a fact he has decided will be true.

"If frying my IMC chip in a standing columnar wave doesn't work," he continues, "I'll try something else. Bresner will help. Jex will help. We won't stop until reality stabilizes."

"And if you can't fix it?" I ask.

Sam meets my eyes.

"Then I'll come back for you," he says. "I'll take you to Lindsay's world. You'll be with her. I swear it."

It hits me harder than I expect—

the idea that he has thought that far ahead,

that he has built a safety net beneath my heartbreak.

I swallow hard.

"Thank you," I say. "For everything.
For giving me a chance to have the unlikeliest of friends.
For letting me meet her."

Sam nods once, like the words land somewhere deep in him.

I roll up my sleeve.

The serum feels cold in my hand.

Final in the way all endings feel final.

"Ready?" Sam asks.

"No," I say. "But do it anyway."

I inject the serum.

The anchoring chemical slides into my bloodstream, lighting
my nerves from the inside. My knees wobble, but I stay
upright.

Sam steps forward and pulls me into a hug—

the kind where a person says more with their arms than they
could ever say out loud.

"You're a real man, Markus," he murmurs. "Don't forget that."

My voice breaks. "You too."

He steps back, raises the device, and the world around him begins to fold inward—

light collapsing like a box closing in on itself,
edges tightening,
color draining to white.

"Goodbye," I say.

But he is already gone.

Just the crackle of displaced air.

Just the shimmer fading.

I stand there alone under the aura-colored sky—

the storm above me shifting and groaning like a living thing—

and for the first time in days, in weeks, maybe in my whole life…

…I feel the weight of my world settle back onto my shoulders.

But I don't break.

Not yet.

Sam is gone.

I am alone.

But something inside me whispers that I won't be alone forever. Not if Sam keeps his promise.

For a few days, I do nothing.

Absolutely nothing.

I go back to my half-broken apartment, collapse on the bed, and let the hours wash over me like dull waves. On the second night, I jolt awake in a panic—heart racing, lungs tight—as if danger has followed me home. For a moment I don't know what year I'm in. I grab the edge of the mattress and wait for the room to stop spinning.

I think of Lindsay.

Wonder if she's okay.

If she's anchored.

If she remembers me.

The panic eventually breaks, the way storms do—slowly, without apology. I breathe, force myself into stillness, and remind myself that Sam says he will fix things. That he has to fix them.

By the third morning, something in me shifts.

Not strength—just momentum, the smallest willingness to stand.

I step outside and look up.

The sky is still wrong.

Still flickering.

Still smeared with the colors of an hour that doesn't belong.

But beneath the chaos… something is moving.

A pull. A pressure.

Like reality taking a deep breath.

I feel it—that backward ripple.

The one Sam talks about.

The one he says will unwind the damage like a film running in reverse, stitching whole the things that time has torn.

If Sam succeeds, the restoration won't come all at once.

It will move backward through years—through every fracture, every consequence, every death—

Fixing everything.

Even the things I never knew were broken.

Days pass. Maybe weeks. I stop counting.

I study physics.

Time mechanics.

Anything that might explain the quiet changes happening around me.

But it isn't the struggle I expect.

It comes easily—almost frighteningly so. Concepts that should take months click in days. Equations unfold in my head like old memories I'm recovering instead of learning. Every principle—entropy flow, interference patterns, oscillation decay—feels connected to something I've already lived through with Sam, Jex, Dr. Bresner, and especially Lindsay.

Jex's voice sticks in my mind whenever I work on field interactions:

"Physics has a soft spot for stubborn men."

And Bresner—his steady, patient intelligence—is there each time I see the elegance hidden in the math:

"Time isn't magic, Markus. It's machinery. And machinery can be repaired."

I take classes—advanced ones, the kind students usually save for much later—but the work doesn't crush me the way it should. It sharpens me. Gives my mind something to hold instead of breaking. I stay late after lectures, helping professors run simulations. Eventually one of them hands me a keycard and says:

"You learn fast. Faster than most grad students. Ever consider working in the lab?"

Awful pay. Long nights.

But I say yes.

I soak in everything—sensor arrays, interference modeling, microwave field behavior. I learn to stabilize waveforms, to read resonance shifts by eye, to build the kind of crude prototypes that might make Jex proud. Sometimes I catch myself smiling at a breakthrough I wish I could show him. Sometimes I whisper a discovery out loud, imagining Bresner nodding, adjusting his glasses, adding something brilliant of his own.

And on the days when the work feels too big, I go back to the place where I used to sit with Lindsay— by the shallow stream. I bring a notebook, sketch equations, watch the sky pulse and shift above me.

It feels like studying in two worlds at once—mine, and the one I hope Sam is still fighting for.

Sometimes the wind moves just right, and I can almost hear her laugh.

Almost feel Sam's calm beside me.

Almost imagine Jex shouting about some new theory that makes no sense at first, but always does eventually.

It keeps me going.

It keeps me believing.

Then one morning—

Everything snaps.

The anomaly vanishes like a curtain dropping.

The sky turns whole.

Blue. Wide. Honest.

The world feels lighter.

Like someone has lifted a weight off its chest.

My heart pounds.

Because I know what that means.

Sam does it.

He fixes the timeline.

I run home.

I hit my street out of breath and nearly collapse when I see
her—

Aunt Carol.

Carrying groceries up the steps, muttering to herself about the price of fruit.

Alive.

Normal.

As if nothing has ever taken her away.

She looks up. "Markus? Honey, what are you doing outside without a jacket?"

My knees almost give out.

I hug her before she can ask anything else.

She laughs, confused, patting my back.

"I'm fine," she says. "I'm right here. Why wouldn't I be?"

Because you were gone, I think.

Because the world broke.

Because Sam stitched it back together.

But I don't say any of that.

I just hold her tighter.

When I step inside—

I hear voices.

Two voices I haven't heard in years.

My parents.

Alive.

Talking.

Laughing.

I freeze in the doorway.

My father looks up. "Hey, kiddo. You okay?"

I nearly collapse.

My mother reaches me first, pulling me into her arms like I've just woken from a nightmare she never knew happened.

"It's okay," she whispers. "You're home."

No one remembers the anomaly.

Not the deaths.

Not the fractures.

Not the terror.

But I remember.

And I know—

If my world is restored,

Lindsay's must be too. I wonder if my parents' deaths were caused by the anomaly's fallout, but it doesn't matter anymore.

That thought hits me like a heartbeat I didn't know I'd lost.

"I'll be right back," I tell my family.

They barely have time to ask where I'm going.

I run.

Run straight to the house where Lindsay once lived.

Hoping.

Praying.

Stupidly believing miracles might come in pairs.

But when I reach the porch—

She isn't there.

A different family lives inside.

A different life.

A different world.

I stand on the sidewalk, breathing the clean new air of a fixed reality, feeling the silence settle around me.

I know it's a shot in the dark.

But still—

I hoped.

I go home after that.

Not because I want to.

Because there is nowhere else to run.

My parents keep hovering, asking if I want dinner, if I feel sick, if something happened at school. I lie with the ease of someone who has lived through too much truth. I tell them I'm tired. That I just need sleep.

That night, I lie awake for hours listening to the small noises of a house that should not exist anymore—my mother moving through the kitchen, my father turning pages in the living room, Aunt Carol humming while she folds laundry. Ordinary sounds that feel like miracles.

And yet underneath all of it, something tugs at me.

A name.

A face.

Lindsay.

She is out there somewhere—I know that—but not here. Not in this repaired version of reality. Not in this world Sam has stitched shut with his own suffering.

I close my eyes and let the thought tear quietly through me.

She's out there.

But not with me.

I drift into sleep sometime after midnight, the ache settling into something dull and steady—the kind of pain you learn to carry because there's no other choice.

The next morning, I walk to the place where Lindsay and I used to talk—the shallow stream on the edge of town, grass bending in long wind-strands, water moving with its slow, patient rhythm. The sky above is still whole, impossibly blue, as if the universe wants to show off what Sam has saved.

A breeze moves through the reeds.

The quiet feels familiar.

Too familiar.

I sit down where we once were—same slant of sun—and the memory of her comes rushing back so sharply it almost buckles me.

I pull in a breath and let it out slowly.

"I hope you're okay," I say to the empty air.

My voice cracks like old paint peeling from a wall.

"I hope your world feels better than this."

I stay there awhile—an hour, maybe more—watching the river curl around stones, watching the light shift along the

water. Time feels stretched thin, like the world hasn't
finished settling after the ripple Sam sent back through it.

Then I feel it.

A pull.

A pressure.

Not the same as the day reality snaps back into place—
something smaller, more precise. Like a thread being tugged
from somewhere just beyond the seam of the world.

I look down at my hand.

At the Mag-C ring Sam gave me.

For months it has been silent steel.

But now—

It radiates.

Just once.

Barely more than a whisper of movement.

My breath catches.

I lift my hand.

The ring pulls again.

Toward the treeline.

Toward the riverbend.

Toward *something.*

Something waiting.

Something calling.

Something that feels like her.

I stand slowly, my heart pounding so hard it makes my fingertips shake.

The ring tugs a third time—

not gentle, not curious.

A pull with intent.

With direction.

With recognition.

I raise my hand.

The metal is warm. Warmer than it has ever been.

And then—

It glows.

Not bright, not intrusive—

but like something waking up after a long sleep.

A soft, golden pulse moves along its edges.

Then comes the sound.

A low hum, barely audible, but I feel it in my bones.

A vibration that matches my heartbeat, then overtakes it.

The air around me thickens, ripples, stretches.

The ring isn't just reacting.

It's answering.

Somewhere—

not here, not now, not in this timeline—

another ring hums back.

Lindsay's.

A connection sparks between them, thin as silk, bright as lightning.

Two points in space pulling toward each other across the fracture Sam has stitched shut.

The field around me bends inward.

Colors fold.

Light warps.

And then—

A tear opens in the air.

A slit in the world, glowing gold along the edges, trembling like a living thing that echoes the same strange glow I see when time bends.

A seam between timelines, held together by two rings trying desperately to reach each other.

I step closer.

My breath catches.

Through the tear, I see a hand.

Small.

Familiar.

Shaking.

Her hand.

"Lindsay," I whisper.

The tear widens when I say her name—like the world itself recognizes the sound.

Her fingers reach for me, barely visible through the distortion, but I would know them in any universe.

Without thinking, without fear, without hesitation—

I reach into the tear.

Warmth surges up my arm, a shock of energy racing through every nerve.

For a heartbeat, I feel two worlds at once—

the grass under my feet,
the wind from hers,
the echo of her breath meeting mine.

Our fingers brush.

Then lock.

Her grip tightens with the kind of strength people only have when they finally find what they feared they have lost forever.

I brace my feet, pull, and the tear flares wide—

a burst of gold, like a wound healing backward.

"Come on," I whisper.

"I've got you."

One more pull—

And Lindsay falls forward into my world, collapsing into my arms as the tear snaps shut behind her with a quiet, final sigh.

She is warm.

Real.

Alive.

Her forehead presses into my shoulder, her breath shaking against my neck.

"Markus," she whispers.

A tremor of disbelief.

Relief.

Home.

The ring cools against my skin.

The field goes silent.

But the world—

my world—

is whole again.

And Lindsay is in it.

Chapter Twelve
Year: 2080 — Samuel

I know something is wrong the second I see Bresner's face. He stands over the core like a priest over a relic, hands folded behind his back, eyes bright in that way that always means he has good news and bad news and no sense of which is which.

"How long?" I ask.

He doesn't pretend not to know what I mean.

"For the planet?" he says. "Years."

He lifts a hand, already bracing for impact. "But, Samuel—it's years with a guarantee instead of months with a coin toss. We can hold the field, damp the drift, bleed off the excess flux from the core–mantle boundary. We can stop the worst of it."

"Years," I repeat. "People are already dying."

"Fewer will," he says. "That's the shape of mercy we're working with."

It isn't enough. Not after everything. Not after dragging two kids through time and handing him a star in a suitcase.

"Show me," I say.

He brightens at that. Scientists always do when you give them a problem instead of a complaint.

Bresner crosses to the containment bay and keys in a code. A slab of glass darkens and then clears, revealing the cold fusion sample nested in its suspension cradle—a small blue sphere inside a transparent cube, latticed with field coils and sensor lines.

"Here," he says. "Scaled model. Think of it as a temper tantrum in a box. We replicate the erratic magnetohydrodynamic flow you'd see in the outer core—convection columns, shearing currents, flux ropes snapping and reconnecting. All the lovely chaos that makes our magnetosphere stutter and cough."

He taps a console. Inside the cube, red filaments writhe through a hazy plasma, arcing and buckling against invisible boundaries. The meters climb, jittery and nervous.

"Uncorrected," he says. "Field variance at twenty-three sigma. No stable dipole. Everything wandering. Everything fraying."

He slides a control.

The cold fusion core wakes.

Blue light spreads from it in thin threads, weaving itself into the chaos like a second thought. The red filaments shudder, then start to straighten, realigning along new lines of force. The meters drop—slow, steady, like a fever breaking.

"Coupled to the right coil geometry," Bresner says, "this thing is a metronome. It drives a clean oscillation into the mess. Forces the turbulent plasma to pick a direction and stick with it. You stabilize the core dynamo, you stabilize the field. Enough of these in the right places and we can pin the magnetosphere back into something civilized."

The last of the red noise vanishes. The readouts settle. The box glows a calm, impossible blue.

"For the planet," he says softly, almost reverent, "this works. I stake my life on that."

Some of the tightness in my chest loosens. I have spent years watching models degrade, simulations fall off cliffs, projections end with the same thin line of extinction. This is the first time I see anything move in the other direction.

"Good," I say. It comes out harsher than I mean. "So you save the planet. Now we fix the timeline."

Bresner's smile falters.

"Ah," he says. "Yes. That."

He shuts down the model; the blue dims back to ordinary glass. The room feels duller without it.

"The planet is physics," he goes on. "Messy, but obedient. The timeline…" He exhales. "The timeline is surgery on the patient that's already walking around."

"Can you remove the chip," I ask, "or fry it and be done?"

He looks at me like a man who has rehearsed this conversation and still hates it.

"Mechanically? Yes. I can excise it. Cut power to the lattice. Or I can do what our friend Titor suggests and hit it with a standing columnar microwave pulse—generate a focused node right where the IMC sits, overdrive the resonant circuits, melt them into silence."

"Then do it."

"It might kill you," he says.

"I don't care."

He ignores that. "And even if it doesn't kill you, and even if it collapses the tether you've created, we have no guarantee that the damage to the larger chronology reverses. We have models. Jex has… colorful arguments." His mouth twitches. "But no trials. No data. Just the hope that if we knock out the anchor, the ripples run backward and smooth themselves."

"That's more than we had yesterday."

"It is also less than you deserve to bet your life on," he says.

I laugh once. "You think my life hasn't already been bet?"

Jex, who's been leaning against a console pretending not to listen, straightens. "Run him through the theory again," he says. "The standing wave."

Bresner rubs his temples, then gestures for me to sit on the stool beside the main array.

"The IMC," he says, "sits in your temporal lobe, bonded to your neural lattice. It talks to the network by emitting and receiving phased bursts—microwave frequency, nested in a carrier pattern. Titor's idea is to trap those emissions in a vertical resonant column—two phased emitters, floor and ceiling—so the wave stands in place instead of propagating."

He mimes a line between his hands.

"You match the resonance to the chip's antenna geometry, overdrive it, and in theory the feedback burns out every time-active component in your skull. No more tether. No more unauthorized jumps. No more you borrowing the universe like a library book."

"Good," I say. "When do we start?"

"Samuel." He sighs. "If it works perfectly, you lose the chip. You lose your access. You might seize. You might forget. You might simply fall over and never get up again."

I meet his eyes. "And if we do nothing, the world stays as it is—all of them. Broken. Split."

He hesitates, then gives the worst part.

"And if it works in the larger sense," he says quietly, "if the timeline truly does knit back together—if this branching catastrophe collapses into a single, healthier history—none of us will know. We won't be able to check. Because you won't be able to travel anymore to see whether Markus's world and Lindsay's world merge or part or carry on without us."

From the corner, Jex frowns. "Wouldn't we know if it worked if our world goes back to normal? Sky clears, anomalies stop, all that?"

Bresner shakes his head. "Not necessarily. Think of it this way: the fracture that produces our world is the same fracture that allows us to reach backward. We are the echo. The repair has to start behind us and move forward. Our timeline—the echo—provides the push, the boundary condition. Even if the primary history is healed, this branch could remain frozen exactly as it is until it winds down."

"So we're the scaffolding," Jex says. "Once the building's fixed, we're still out here, bolted to nothing."

"Exactly," Bresner says. "We might never know whether the surgery succeeded. We could save them and still be stuck in the ruined wing, sweeping up glass."

I let that sit between us.

"You're telling me," I say slowly, "that I can let you fry this thing in my head, maybe die, maybe live, maybe fix the universe—and from where I'm standing, nothing changes."

"More or less," Bresner says. "Ethically speaking, it's a nightmare. Mathematically speaking, it's elegant."

I stare at the dark glass of the containment bay. At the empty cradle where the core was. At my reflection, thin and tired and already halfway erased.

"I don't care if I know," I say. "I care that they get a world that's whole."

"Sam—" Jex starts.

I cut him off with a raised hand. "You told Markus you'd try for a backward ripple. You told Lindsay you'd break the calendar for her if you had to. I'm there."

"I know what I told them," Jex says quietly.

"And I know what I owe them," I say.

Silence falls again. The machines hum. Somewhere, a cooling fan kicks on, like the lab is sighing.

Bresner finally nods. "It's your head," he says. "Your life. I won't pretend I'm not curious to see what happens."

He starts checking settings, murmuring to himself, circuits and power levels and safe thresholds that don't exist.

Anger rises—at none of them, not really. At the situation. At a universe that thinks it can offer me a choice that isn't a choice at all.

"Give me a minute," I say.

"Of course," Bresner replies. "I'll... recalibrate. We need the emitters aligned to within a millimeter anyway." His mood lightens, as if technical precision is a comfort. It probably is. "Take your time, Samuel. For what it's worth, I am glad you came back."

He turns away, already humming some tuneless fragment as he bends over his instruments.

I walk out.

The corridor feels too narrow, the air too clean. I push through the blast door and step into the dry light outside the facility.

The sky over 2080 is still wrong—colors smeared at the edges, auroral curtains ghosting in places they don't belong. But there's a hint of steadiness now, faint as a pulse returning after a long absence. Bresner's work already picking a fight with the chaos.

I sit on the concrete step, pull out the pack I keep pretending I've quit, and light one with shaking hands.

Jex joins me a moment later and sits without asking.

"So," he says, "we're really going to cook your brain in a microwave column."

"That the technical term?" I ask.

"Close enough."

We smoke in silence for a while, listening to the soft, constant hum of the lab behind us.

"You don't have to do this," Jex says eventually.

"Yeah," I say. "I do."

He nods like he knew that before he asked.

Inside, through the narrow window, I see Bresner moving around the lab, still humming, still working, already arranging the machinery that might stop time from eating itself—by eating my part in it first.

We stub out the cigarettes and go back inside. The lab lights feel harsher now, buzzing with that sickly hum you only hear when a machine's been running too long without rest. Bresner is already moving across the room in quick little lines, muttering to himself, hands full of one thing or another.

He doesn't look up when we enter.

"Good," he says. "You're back. I need both of you."

"For what?" Jex asks.

"A miracle," Bresner says, and finally turns. His eyes are bright again, the way they get when he's three steps ahead of the rest of us. "Cold fusion on the planetary scale isn't a one-man show. I need parts. High-precision coils. Cryo-stabilizers. A microwave resonator that hasn't rotted in the last twenty years. And an inertial dampener from the old defense program."

I frown. "That means going into the cities."

"Yes," Bresner says lightly. "Most surveillance systems collapsed with the magnetosphere. The rest are blind or dying. If there was ever a time to steal from the ruins, it's now."

"It's dangerous," Jex says.

"Samuel," he replies, "everything is dangerous. Breathing is dangerous now. Pick your poison."

We go.

The cities look hollowed out, like something has eaten the insides and left the shells standing out of habit. Towers lean against each other like drunks. Windows flicker with dead screens still trying to report numbers to networks that no longer exist. A few drones hang in the air, lights dim, rotors stuttering like they're dreaming of flight.

We move fast.

Into an abandoned research lab where every drawer stands open, every notebook half-burned.

Into a military base that smells of rust and ozone.

Into a bunker where a single emergency light still blinks at a slow, hopeless rhythm.

We find what we need, though. Coils sealed in vacuum packs. Stabilizers intact. A resonator that takes both of us to pry off the wall. The inertial dampener is buried under a collapsed ceiling panel; Jex spots the corner sticking out like a bone.

When we return to the lab, Bresner looks at the pile like it's a feast and he has been starving.

"You did well," he says. Then he sees my face. "Samuel... sit."

"I'm fine."

"You look as if the world asked for one more pound of flesh and you're running out of places to cut," he says. "Sit."

I sit.

He pulls up a portable array, his fingers dancing across the interface.

"I need you to jump," he says.

"Now?"

"Just out and back. Fifteen seconds. I need to capture the emission profile from your IMC during a clean transition—microwave harmonics, chronon bleed, the local shear signature." He smiles faintly. "I peek at the readings from your last uncontrolled jump. Fascinating. But messy."

"You sure it's safe?" Jex asks.

"No," Bresner says. "But it'll be quick."

I stand, breathe once, feel that familiar pull in the back of my skull—the capsule behind my left ear, the lattice whispering, the universe ready to split open under my feet.

Then I'm gone.

Then I'm back.

The whole thing takes less time than a man takes to blink in disbelief.

Bresner nearly dances.

"Yes. Yes! I get it. Every trace particle. Every pulse. Samuel, someday this may help us tame this thing. Controlled temporal displacement. The way it should have been from the start."

I don't like the sound of that.

"Time travel has done enough."

"As a species," he says softly, "we clean up messes we don't understand. That's the curse of being human."

I don't argue. Maybe because he's right.

A month passes.

We sleep in shifts, eat from ration packs that taste like warm chalk. Outside, the sky flickers with colors that don't belong to any season. The planet is getting sicker. The sunrises look bruised.

During that month, Jex and I talk—more than we have in years, maybe ever.

"What if," he says once, "we go back further? Fix things. Not just this. Other stuff. Things that broke long before us."

"No," I say.

"You don't even know what I'm asking."

"I know what it costs."

"It could change everything."

"It could ruin everything," I say. "You don't fix a shattered mirror by punching it again."

He looks angry for a while. Then tired.

We let the topic die between us.

Early one morning, Bresner walks out of the fabrication bay holding a small cylinder, frost clinging to its edges, glowing faint blue from within.

"It's ready," he whispers.

The cold fusion deterrent prototype.

It hums faintly—an unborn star packed tight in metal and equations.

Now comes the hard part.

We've spent that month carving a narrow descent path—a resonance shaft bored into the mantle's fractures using micro-drills and harmonic boring rigs. We're not reaching the core physically; that's impossible. But we've created a stabilized conduit straight to the outer core boundary where the deterrent field can propagate.

Believable? Maybe not for the old world. For this one—broken and screaming—it's the best anyone can do.

We take the device to the mouth of the shaft.

Bresner gives it one last look, presses the arming switch, and lets it go.

The drop is silent.

The aftermath isn't.

The ground trembles.

The air thickens.

Every instrument in the lab spikes, then starts to slide toward stability like a frantic heart finding its rhythm.

Inside, the readouts shift from angry red to cold green.

"It's working," Bresner whispers. "God help us. It's actually working."

I let out a breath I don't realize I've been holding for years.

Jex grabs me, pulls me into a tight hug.

I hug him back.

Then we both turn to Bresner and pull him in too.

He stiffens like a man unused to being touched, then gives up and lets it happen.

For a moment, we're not scientists, or survivors, or time thieves.

We're just people who've saved a world.

Then reality comes back.

"What about the timeline?" I ask.

The light drains from Bresner's face.

"I've been working on that too," he says. "Every night. Comparing the particles I captured from your jump with the anomalies scattered worldwide. Matching signatures. Tracking fractures."

"And?"

He rubs his eyes.

"There's nothing to fix."

"What do you mean nothing?"

"I mean the break is permanent. The chronology has branched too far. The original causal path is inaccessible. No standing wave will reverse it. It won't collapse the branches. It won't stitch anything together. All it will do is burn out your IMC and kill you."

Jex stares at him. "You're sure?"

"Yes," he says.

Something inside me loosens—not relief. Something emptier.

"So that's it?" I ask.

"That's it," he says gently.

I leave the lab. Jex tries to follow, but I tell him no. I need to be alone.

I walk past the dome, out to the thin woods beyond where the air smells like old pine and static. I sit on a fallen trunk and listen to the wind move through the branches like a voice too tired to speak.

I think about Markus pacing my living room, refusing to accept the truth.

Lindsay crying into her hands.

Jex shouting in the truck.

Juliette laughing in the sunlight like it belongs to her.

I have failed every one of them in one timeline or another.

Maybe this is the only choice left.

I walk back.

They know the moment they see me.

Bresner closes his laptop.

Jex steps forward.

"No," he says.

"Yes," I tell him.

"You don't have to do this."

"I do."

Jex grabs my arm, hard.

"You're just going to leave us? Leave me?"

I pull him in and hold him, for the first time without hesitation.

He holds on like a man drowning.

"You're the best part of this ruined world," he says against my shoulder.

"You too," I say. "But some things you can't fix. Some things you can only meet."

I let him go.

I turn to Bresner.

"Take care of him," I say.

Bresner nods once, solemn. "I will."

I step back, feel the IMC hum, feel the air thin, feel the universe open its old familiar wound.

I look at both of them.

Identity wave confirmation.
Select date on calendar file.
Direct reset.
Pulse wave to my IMC chip.
Phone lights up.
Time travel initiates.

"Tell Markus and Lindsay they deserved better," I say. "Tell them I tried."

"Sam—" Jex chokes.

But I'm already gone.

Into 2079.

Toward Juliette.

Toward whatever ending waits for us there.

The world catches me by the throat and shakes.

Heat.

Light.

The thin metallic taste of the city's air.

I'm back.

It takes a second for my head to stop ringing. When it does, I know exactly where I am.

The transit platform.

The day I go to pick Juliette up.

Her last day.

People move past me in fast, blurred lines—late commuters, workers, kids with packs hanging off one shoulder. The same announcements echo off the concrete, the same chime before a train arrives, the same vibration under my boots.

The day hasn't changed.

I have.

I know how this day ends. Where the sky tears. Where the first anomalies bloom and eat a piece of the world. Where she dies.

I come back to die with her.

The mag-line slides into the station on a cushion of humming air. Doors sigh open. A few people step off. A few step on. I move with them, hand on the rail, like I've done it a thousand times.

Inside, the car is almost empty.

That's wrong.

Morning runs are usually packed—standing room only, shoulders and elbows and bored faces trying not to see each other. Now there are only a handful of figures scattered through the car. Then the chime sounds again, the doors close, and one by one they blur and are… gone.

Like someone is cutting frames out of a film.

I blink.

When my eyes clear, there are only two people left on the mag-transport.

Me.

And the stranger from the cemetery.

He sits three rows down, by the window. Same black coat. Same thin wrists. Same clean, unreadable face. Young—

maybe a few years under me. In my memory he was older;
when grief remembers someone, it adds weight they didn't
have.

He notices me looking.

He smiles once, small and polite, then stands. The car hums
as it accelerates out of the station, the city sliding past in
glass and steel. He walks down the aisle and sits directly
across from me.

No one comes to scan my retina. No conductor walks
through. No announcements. Just the steady, low song of
the mag-field and the stranger's eyes on mine.

"Hello, Samuel," he says.

My mouth goes dry. "We've met."

"At your parents' graves," he says. "You're very polite."

"You followed me here?"

He tilts his head, like he's listening to a question I haven't
asked.

"I go where I'm needed," he says. "Today that happens to be
this line."

Out the window, the city rolls by, half asleep and unaware. I
glance up the aisle again. Every seat empty. No cameras
blinking. No ticket drones.

"This is wrong," I say. "It's never this empty."

"True," he says.

"And the staff—"

"There aren't any today," he says simply. "Well, at the moment."

He folds his hands in his lap, like a student waiting for class to begin.

"What are you?" I ask.

"Complicated," he says. "But you know me already."

"I don't," I say.

"You do," he says, almost gently. "In the ways that matter. You know I'm not here to hurt you. You know I'm here because today matters."

Outside, the sky looks normal. Blue, thin clouds, sun trying to burn through the haze. Somewhere above all that, I know, the fractures are forming—the same fault lines Bresner spends his life chasing in equations.

"So," he goes on. "You're going back to her."

"Yes."

"To die with her."

"Yes."

He nods once, like that confirms something on a list.

"Why?" he asks.

"Because I owe her that much."

"That's not an answer," he says calmly. "Owing is a ledger. I'm asking about love."

I almost laugh.

"You picked the wrong train for philosophy," I say.

"There are no wrong trains," he says. "Only late passengers. Tell me, Samuel: what do you do for someone you care about that deeply?"

I look at him. The car rocks softly as it curves along the eastern ring. The city opens up below us—rooftops, parks, the thin thread of a river.

"I die for them," I say.

"That's the easy part," he says.

"Easy," I repeat.

"Dying is one decision," he says. "One moment. One act. What else do you do?"

I think of Markus shouting in my living room.

Lindsay crying.

The way I cut them out of my plans because the truth would have broken them.

"I stay away if I have to," I say slowly. "If it keeps them safe. If it makes them happy. I stay apart from them for the rest of my life if that's what it takes."

He studies my face like he's inspecting a fracture for hairline cracks.

"Even if they never know," he says. "Even if they think you don't care."

"Yes."

"Even if it means you die alone."

"Yes," I say.

He leans back. A faint, satisfied light touches his eyes.

"That's closer," he says quietly.

Something in my chest eases. Not because anything is better, but because the words are out now, hanging between us like a confession in a quiet church.

"Do you ever doubt it?" he asks.

"The love?" I say.

He nods.

"No," I say. "I doubt everything else. The math. The jumps. The choices. The so-called plan. But not that."

"Why not?"

"I just know," I say.

He smiles.

Outside, the track arches over the river. I watch sunlight scatter off the water, bright and hard.

"I've seen many people make claims like that," he says. "I've seen some die for less. I've seen some run from more. You, though… you keep walking back into the fire."

"Maybe I'm bad at learning."

"Or maybe you're stubborn in the right direction."

He glances at the ceiling, listening again to something I can't hear.

"Our stop is coming," he says.

I look up. No station announcements. No chime. Just the steady rush of air and the numbers on the overhead display ticking toward the transfer hub where I meet Juliette's route.

"What do you call what you're doing?" he asks. "Right now. Today. Going to her."

"Dying," I say. "With good company."

He shakes his head.

"Love," he says softly. "That's the word that fits."

The mag-line begins to decelerate. The city tilts as we
approach the next platform. The stranger stands.

He smooths his coat with thin hands, then looks down at me
for the last time.

"You have my grace," he says.

He turns toward the door as the car slides into the station.

"Wait—" I start. I stand up.

The doors hiss open.

The world floods back.

A wave of commuters pours in—voices, bags, perfume, the
angry buzz of a man on a call, a kid laughing too loud. The
empty car fills in three heartbeats. I shove against them,
craning my neck, trying to find the black coat, the thin
wrists, the calm face.

Nothing.

He's gone.

A conductor shoulders past me, scanning tickets, calling out
the line number. A drone flicks its lights in my face and
chirps for retinal validation. The overhead display blinks a
delayed arrival notice and a weather alert, like everything has
always been this normal.

I step back, dazed, and let the crowd carry me inside. The
doors shut. The train lurches forward.

For a long stretch I just stand there, hanging on to the rail, watching my reflection shiver in the glass. I feel like a man who has stepped out of a dream into another dream and can't find the seam.

I don't know what "grace" means, not really. Only that it feels like something has shifted under my feet.

My wrist buzzes.

Her ID lights up on the contact plate.

"Hey," I say, and my voice almost breaks.

"Hey yourself," Juliette says. "You on your way?"

"Yeah," I say. "I'm almost there."

"Good. I, uh…" I hear a small rustle, a bag being moved. "I found persimmons in the market. The real kind, not the synth crap. I got us some. I thought we could sit somewhere and eat them. Like civilized people for once."

A laugh catches in my chest.

"Persimmons," I say.

"Don't sound so suspicious," she says. "They're just fruit, Sam."

"Nothing about you is 'just' anything," I say.

She makes a small, embarrassed noise. "You're weird today."

"It's a weird day."

"See you soon," she says.

"Yeah," I say. "See you soon."

The call ends.

You know how the rest of it goes.

The meeting spot. The way she leans against the rail, black hair pulled back, tattoos showing when our fingers interlock. The little box burning a hole in my pocket. The stupid, nervous jokes. Her hand slipping into mine when she thinks no one is looking.

Only this time, I feel everything like my skin has been torn off.

The ride.

The curve of the road out of the city.

The sky, already a shade too bright at the edges.

We park where we always park when we want to pretend the world is gentler than it is—a narrow turnout off a service road, near a stretch of trees that somehow survived all the zoning committees.

We walk down to the stream.

The water is low—just a thin body of clear liquid over smooth stones, tadpoles flicking like commas near the bank. The air smells of damp earth and leaves.

Juliette spreads a worn blanket on the ground, sits cross-legged, and opens the bag. Three persimmons roll out, bright and heavy.

"Behold," she says. "A miracle of agriculture."

I sit beside her.

Up above, the first ripple cuts across the sky—a band of color bending the blue. People in the city are probably looking up already, making recordings, sending panicked messages.

I don't.

I watch her instead.

She bites into a persimmon, juice running down her wrist. "Oh," she says. "Oh, that's good. Here."

She presses one into my hand. The flesh is soft, sweet. It tastes like late summers I never have.

She catches me staring.

"What?" she asks.

"Nothing."

"Liar."

I swallow, wipe my hand on my pants, and turn to face her.

"Juliette," I say.

She feels the shift and goes still.

"How do you even know you love me, Sam?" she asks quietly. "What if it's just... something else—pressure, adrenaline, the moment?"

I smile, because she picks the exact question that has been sitting in my chest since the day I met her.

"I know because I know," I say.

She frowns. "That's not an answer."

"It's the only one that fits," I say. "I've second-guessed every choice I've made. Every move. Every plan. Every decision. But not this. Not you."

She looks down at her hands. A drop of juice falls to the blanket.

"What if you're wrong?" she asks. Her voice is very small. "What if you've mistaken it for something bigger than it is?"

"I don't mistake you for anything," I say. "When I say I love you, it's the one part of my life that isn't guesswork. You're the one thing I don't doubt. I love you. I know it the way I know the ground is under me—without doubt."

She lets out a breath I don't realize she's been holding. Her eyes shine, not with the wild light of panic or the sharp anger

I've seen so many times, but with something softer. Something that has been waiting a long time to come out.

She leans forward and presses her forehead to mine.

"Okay," she whispers. "Okay."

We sit like that for a long moment, the world narrowing to the sound of the stream and the birds and her breathing.

Another ripple rolls across the sky.

The trees whisper as the wind moves through them, carrying that warm, late-summer hush that settles instead of stirs. The air unusual for a moment—just enough for me to notice, just enough to make the IMC stir faintly at the base of my skull. It doesn't whine or pulse the way it used to. No tug. No static. No sense of bending reality around me.

Just a soft, fading hum.

Like whatever power I have is slipping loose, draining out, or maybe just turning itself off.

I can't say for sure.

But it doesn't run through my head the same way anymore.

A part of me wonders if that's the point—an ending inside another ending.

Juliette doesn't notice any of it. She sits with her knees pulled up, watching the sky lighten at the edges as the sun lowers.

"It should start soon," she says.

"What should?" I ask, knowing but wanting to hear her say it.

She smiles. "The fireflies. My dad said they show up right before the real dark hits. I haven't seen them in years. I want you to see them too."

No talk of danger.

No fear of the sky tearing.

No shadow of what I remember.

Just her waiting for something simple and beautiful.

We lie back on the blanket, shoulders touching, the stream whispering beside us. The clouds overhead drift in long, ordinary strokes—not twisted, not bending, not glowing with the sickness of a fractured world. Just clouds.

The anomaly is gone.

The sky holds the way it should have held all along.

Juliette breathes out softly. "This is nice."

"Yeah, it is."

She turns her head toward me. "You're different today."

"Different how?"

"Just… sure," she says. "Like you decided something."

I look at her, at the softness of the moment she doesn't know we could have lost, and everything in my chest tightens with something like grief and gratitude woven together.

"It's the only one that fits," I say. "I've second-guessed every choice I've made. Every move. Every plan. Every decision. But not this. Not you."

Her eyes soften, a warmth rising behind them.

Before she can answer, a faint glow flickers at the treeline.

Juliette shoots upright. "There—look!"

More lights follow—tiny gold sparks drifting between the branches, pulsing gently in the growing dark. One blinks above the stream, another near Juliette's knee, then a dozen more.

Fireflies, bright and warm, moving like small lanterns carried by an invisible breeze.

Juliette laughs under her breath. "See? Told you. Magic."

I watch one drift past my hand, its glow flaring, dimming, flaring again.

For a second, the pattern reminds me of time-jump light— the way reality used to peel back in flashes when I slipped through it.

Except this isn't violent.

It isn't fractured.

It isn't tearing anything apart.

It's gentle.

Natural.

Alive.

Juliette leans against me, her head on my shoulder, watching the warm lights pulse in and out of the dusk.

"They're beautiful," she whispers.

"Yeah, they really are."

The fireflies drift through the trees, blinking in soft patterns that feel like breathing—slow and steady—filling the clearing with a peace I haven't felt in years.

My IMC stays quiet.

The sky stays whole.

And somewhere in the back of my mind I think of the ones who steer me this far—Bresner, Markus, Lindsay, Jex, or that stranger on the mag-line. I don't know which one I owe anything to. I only know I am grateful in that small, wordless way that never asks for anything back.

As the night settles around us, the moment doesn't feel fragile or borrowed.

It feels like it finally belongs.

Because it does.

The universe turns,
and drags me from your orbit,
I have to go.

Epilogue

My mornings come as natural as the creases in the mirror. Not from stress, but from a trail of good memories. I've learned that life is best digested one sip at a time.

"Sam," Juliette says, smiling without looking back, "can you set the table?"

She stands at the stove, butter melting slowly in the saucepan.

"Yeah, of course, my love," I reply, rising from the couch.

"Just two?"

"Just two."

She pauses, glancing toward the window, the yard beyond it.

"I really think we should start planting the watermelons and strawberries farther away from the melons and blueberries," she says. "Our crops look too bunched up."

"We can take care of it soon," I say. "My love."

Juliette cracks the first egg, letting it fall neatly into the hole cut from the bread. *Eggs in the window*, she calls them. I disagree.

"I can't wait to have some eggs in the basket," I announce proudly.

She laughs softly. "I don't know what that is, sweetie. But I *am* making eggs in the window."

She slides the pan slightly, careful not to break the yolk.

"It's just bread with a hole," I say.

"It's breakfast," she replies. "And if you burn the edges, it ruins the whole thing."

"I'm not touching it," I say. "You're the professional."

She sprinkles a little salt over the eggs like it matters more than it probably does. The smell of butter fills the room. Outside, something moves through the leaves. Nothing urgent.

She sets the plates carefully, setting one in front of me, then the other.

"Eat it while it's hot," she says.

I do. The yolk breaks and runs into the bread the way it's supposed to.

"This is good," I say.

"I know," she replies.

We sit together, eating, saying almost nothing, sharing brief glances that say enough.